As his lips touched hers, she closed her eyes.

Tory Emerson had been kissed once or twice before. They had been furtive, inept kisses delivered by infatuated young men from whom she had struggled to escape. This kiss was nothing at all like them. For one thing, it was warm and tender and accomplished. And although it did not threaten her, it was insistent. Far from wanting to escape it, Tory was having the greatest difficulty keeping her hands by her sides, when she really wanted to put her arms around his neck—melt against him. When he raised his head at last and she slowly opened her eyes, she saw a light deep in his gray ones. She put her fingertips to her lips in awe.

By Barbara Hazard
Published by Fawcett Books:

MONDAY'S CHILD
TUESDAY'S CHILD
WEDNESDAY'S CHILD
THURSDAY'S CHILD
FRIDAY'S CHILD

FRIDAY'S CHILD

Barbara Hazard

FAWCETT CREST • NEW YORK

A Fawcett Crest Book
Published by Ballantine Books
Copyright © 1995 by Barbara Hazard

Library of Congress Catalog Card Number: 95-90420

ISBN 0-449-22319-1

Manufactured in the United States of America

First Edition: October 1995

10 9 8 7 6 5 4 3 2 1

"Friday's child is loving and giving."

For Joan Wolf
and in loving memory of
Jewlene Jones

... Friday's children

Monday's child is fair of face,
   Tuesday's child is full of grace.
Wednesday's child is full of woe,
   Thursday's child has far to go.
Friday's child is loving and giving,
   Saturday's child works hard for its living.
And the child that is born on the Sabbath day,
   Is fair and wise and good and gay.
                    —Quoted by A. E. Bray
                    Traditions of Devonshire

Prologue

On a morning in late March, the slightly shabby breakfast room at Lythford Priory was bright and cheerful. It was true the hangings at the large bow window were faded, but they had faded well, their colors softening and blending in harmony. The old-fashioned Queen Anne furniture had been lovingly cared for over the years, and the ancient carpet beneath the mahogany table, although worn in places, still glowed with muted color. Several covered dishes set over spirit lamps sat on the sideboard, although both occupants of the room had long since pushed away the remains of their breakfasts to peruse their morning post.

The elderly lady who sat at one end of the table stifled a gasp as she read a long letter, and the tear that crept down her wrinkled cheek was followed shortly by another, and then another. Surreptitiously she wiped them away with her napkin.

"What's that fool woman been writing to you now, to make you cry, Martha?" the equally elderly gentleman opposite her demanded as he looked up and caught her at it. "I don't know why you correspond with Mrs. Hawley, when her letters invariably send you into the mopes for a week."

"I'm sorry. I did not mean to cry," she said. "It's just her news is so very unfortunate . . ."

"Napoleon has escaped again? The king is dead? Plague is sweeping London? The banks have failed?"

"You must not jest about such things, Roger," she said, her kind old voice as stern as she could make it. "It is not at all well-done of you. And you know it is none of those things."

"Then, let me guess. She writes of Nicholas, does she not? What has the young idiot been up to this time?"

"How on earth did you know it was about him?" his sister demanded, looking astounded in spite of her distress.

"Her letters almost always feature him. Sometimes I think your dear, *dear* friend does nothing but follow the man around, waiting for him to do one more outrageous thing so she can hasten to report it to you. Embellished, I am sure, with a great many flourishes and conjectures of her own. Ninny!"

"It is true she is too fond of gossip, but what you say of her is not kind, brother . . ."

"Kind?" he snorted, using his napkin to remove any crumbs that might have been caught in his bristling white mustache. "I've never been kind. Damned waste of time. But forget that. What did she say?"

"That this time Nicky has gone too far, even by the most lax standards. Everyone in the ton is talking about him."

Her brother snorted again, and she hurried on, "It is not because he has set up yet another extravagant mistress. It is because he lost ten thousand pounds last week in only one evening of play. Oh, I wish cards had never been invented!"

"But still, he'd be able to wager on dice or horse

2

races or the Fancy, now, wouldn't he?" her brother asked dryly.

"Roger, there must be something we can do to stop him before he runs through his entire fortune! There must be," his sister said, returning to the heart of the matter.

"What? There's nothing we can do, old girl," the elderly gentleman said, sounding genuinely sorry that it was so. "He's the head of his family now, and at the age of twenty-eight, his own man. We are only relatives from his mother's side. If I thought it would do any good, I'd ask him down to Lythford, but we both know it wouldn't make any difference. Even if he bothered to come."

"He always does so, except when he has other plans he cannot change," his sister reminded him. "You know he is not rude."

"No, his manners are quite possibly the only good thing about him. But haven't you noticed how very often he has other plans?"

"Nicky is a young man. It cannot be amusing for him, visiting two old fogies like us."

"If you are content to consider yourself such a thing, Martha, you are welcome to do so, but I am not, nor have I any intentions of ever becoming, an old fogy. I'll thank you to remember it.

"However, we stray from the subject. I can excuse many things in my great-nephew; indeed, I have often done so in the past, but I admit this incessant wagering he seems determined to engage in worries me. And it is strange, too. He never used to take such a fiendish delight in it. It is as if he has suddenly become obsessed, as some men do with drink or women or sport."

He clasped his large, bony hands on the table before him and looked down at them, to hide the bleak concern in his eyes from his sister. Things were bad. Worse than she imagined, as he knew from a letter of his own that he had had in response to various inquiries he had recently set afoot. It was true his great-nephew was wealthy, but no one could live as he was doing and expect to escape the River Tick.

"Perhaps he does it to forget all the sadness he has known," his sister remarked. "It was only after the deaths that he began to gamble heavily, if you recall."

"And wench and drink and drive like a madman. No, the life he has been leading hardly qualifies as mourning. Far from it. And that sad time was four long years ago.

"But that is neither here nor there." He pushed back his chair and rose. He was a tall old man, hardly bowed by the sum of his seventy-two years, and he still had an air of the military about him. General Sir Roger Lincoln had been a man to reckon with before his retirement from the army. Some felt he was that man still.

"Perhaps if you wrote to him, warned him," his sister persisted as he strode to the door.

"Wouldn't do a bit of good. Never has," he said tersely. "Besides, only get his back up. You know his pride."

"Then, I shall have to do what I can," she said softly to herself.

Sir Roger stopped, his hand on the doorknob. As he turned to face her, he said, his voice curiously gentle, "Do you really think praying for the boy will do any good? Think, Martha! How many hours have you spent already on your knees, pleading for that ungrateful scamp? And what has it ever ac-

4

complished? Save your prayers for someone more deserving!"

"But surely you can see deserving people do not need them, while Nicky most certainly does."

He threw up his hands. "I admit defeat. You've rolled me up, foot and guns, my dear. You shall do exactly as you please, of course."

Shaking his head at her, he left the room. Martha Lincoln rang for the butler before she poured herself another cup of coffee. When the servant appeared, she ordered the dogcart brought around immediately.

The butler bowed and went away, well aware of the lady's destination, even though she had not mentioned it. Besides being dearly loved by everyone who knew her for her kindness and goodness, his mistress was also a pious woman who spent much time at church.

Several minutes later, attired in a shawl and her second best bonnet, Martha Lincoln climbed into the dogcart and waved the groom away. She was driving her donkey, an animal that occasionally could be very stubborn.

This morning it set off amiably enough, and it did not need her touch on the reins to know it must turn left toward the village as they left the gates of the priory. Like the butler, the donkey knew her ways.

As she bowled along, Miss Lincoln breathed deeply of the fresh spring air. There was a softness to it this morning that promised the warmth to come. Of course, it was too early for flowers, although the snowdrops had come and gone some weeks before. She told herself she was only imagining a flush of green in the verge and hedgerows, and she glanced up at the blue sky instead, inspecting it for clouds. Roger had said it would rain before nightfall.

She sighed, wishing he were not such a pessimist. Surely enough horrid things happened in life without predicting them all the time. Now, she herself was different. She expected only good. She pondered, not for the first time, how she and her brother had been content to keep house all these years, when they were so temperamentally disparate.

Martha Lincoln was a spinster by choice. She could still remember her father's rage when she refused the young man he had chosen for her. She had often thought it sad she was a Protestant. If she had not been, she would have taken the veil, entering the convent with joy in her vocation. She had never told her brother of this, for he would have been horrified. Like most Anglicans, Roger had no use for the Catholic faith, even scoffing at the vicar when he became too "high" for his taste.

But Martha would have welcomed the rituals: the incense and chanting, the candles and Mass, holy water and confession. And telling her beads would have comforted her.

She was recalled to the present when the little donkey halted of its own accord in some shade near the church door. She got down, talking to it as she tied it to a handy branch. The donkey stood patiently, watching her with its big, dark eyes.

Inside the cool quiet of the church, Miss Lincoln waited for her eyes to adjust to the dim light before she made her way to the pew. She saw she was alone, and for that she was grateful. She had serious supplication to make this morning, and she did not care to be distracted, either by the organist or the vicar.

In the family pew she adjusted the kneeling bench before she sank down on it and clasped her hands before her. All around her was the smell of the old stone building, a smell reminiscent of burning wax, aging hymnals, and mildewed velvet cushions. Her eyes sought the altar with its gold cross and tall candlesticks. Above it, the large stained-glass window depicting the Passion of Christ glowed softly. Martha Lincoln sighed.

She closed her eyes and bent her head. She could have prayed at home, but somehow she felt closer to God in church. And what she had to ask was so important! Her great-nephew had always had a special place in her heart; indeed, she had adored him as the grandson she had never had. Watching fondly as he grew up, she had admired him as a young man, wept when he was hurt, and smiled when he was happy. It was not that she thought he could do no wrong. Dear me, no. She knew very well the wrong he could do. It was why she was here.

She began to pray with all the fervor she could summon. She prayed for divine intervention to save her Nicky from himself. Prayed he would forego his wicked ways, stop gambling and wasting his life in drink and women; begin to have a care for his titles and his name. Prayed that God would help him.

But as she did so, she was nagged by the realization that the Lord helps those who help themselves. It was something she had been taught as a child. She had always believed it.

Of course, it was true, she admitted. But surely there were times when the Lord intervened for people who could not, or would not, help themselves? Surely it only required someone's great faith and constant devotion and petition? Surely He would

One

NICK SINCLAIR WAS tired. Tired, annoyed, short-tempered. He had spent the day at a boxing match near Cliveden, but instead of staying with his cronies in one of the villages nearby, he had decided to make for London instead. The moon was almost full, and it was warm for April. Besides, Lucy was there. Glorious, luscious, *carnal* Lucy. She had been his mistress for only two weeks. Not nearly enough time for her infinite variety to have ceased to enthrall him. Otherwise he would have gone to bed in the country like a sensible man.

Instead he had had an accident. He had not seen what had frightened the horses, but he had his hands full now controlling them. The lights of some small village could be plainly seen ahead, and he snarled an order to his tiger. The lad obeyed as quickly as he could, but even with Sinclair's iron hands on the reins, he could not seem to calm the snorting, rearing team.

"Whoa, I say! Steady there!" the marquess roared, which only disturbed the team further. "Henry, what's the matter? Get the bridles at once!"

Although the tiger did his best, he was no match for the excited horses, and all he got for his pains was stepped on. Crying out in pain, he released the team and hopped away.

The marquess saw his predicament, but he could not go to his aid, not with the horses acting up the way they were doing. "Damn Fotheringham!" he muttered as he struggled with them. "He's the one to blame for their disposition! Got a temper like a fiend. Never should have purchased them for him."

"Can *I* help, guv?" a high, light voice inquired, and the marquess looked down to where a young lad stood in the road. He had no time to wonder why such a child was still abroad this late at night. Instead he said curtly, "Run to the inn. Bring me an ostler!"

"No need for that, guv," the lad said cheerfully. "I'll take them in hand for you."

Before the marquess could protest, for he did not want two crippled children on his hands, the boy moved to the horses' heads. Sinclair could hear him talking to them, although he could not make out the words. And then to his amazement, they ceased bucking and whinnying and settled down as if nothing at all had happened.

"All's well, guv," the boy said. "They won't try to run away now. Er, shouldn't you be looking after your servant?"

Stung, Sinclair jumped from the chaise and went to where his tiger was holding his foot in both hands, rocking back and forth with pain, and sobbing.

"I'm sorry, Henry," he said as he picked the boy up in his arms. "I know it must hurt like the devil, but we'll soon have a doctor for it, and you'll feel better.

"You, there! Do you think you can bring the chaise to the village for me? I must get help for this lad."

" 'Course," the other drawled. "The inn's but a
10

short distance away, up ahead on the left. You go on. I'll bring the rig safe after."

The marquess did not hesitate. Henry was still sobbing, and he was feeling a little guilty about the accident. If he had not been so determined to reach London and Lucy tonight, none of this would have happened. Because if it hadn't been dark, he would have seen what alarmed the team and been able to avoid it. And if he had not been traveling at such a speed, Henry wouldn't be injured now. The guilt did nothing for his temper.

Raising his voice when he reached the inn yard, he soon had a servant running for the doctor, while the innkeeper's wife ordered the maids to prepare a bed and put the kettle on to boil. The innkeeper himself, not at all averse to being roused from a bed he had only just climbed into, brought the marquess a mug of home-brewed, and assured him the best room would be prepared for him at once. There was not much custom at the Oxen's Yoke. He was delighted to be of service.

The marquess watched as Henry was carried tenderly away, then turned to search the road beyond the yard. Sure enough, the young boy was leading the team and chaise into it, and from what he could see, neither had taken any harm from the incident.

Leaving the obsequious host in mid-sentence, he went to greet the boy. In the light of the flambeaux on either side of the inn door, he saw that although he was short and slender, he was older than he had at first appeared. His head was covered with a mass of untidy red curls, and his round face sported a wealth of freckles. Sinclair was sure he had never seen anyone so bran-faced in his life, and it was all he could do not to chuckle. Then the lad smiled at him, and when he saw that gap-toothed grin, he could not help chuckling after all.

"I know. Look something, don't I?" the lad said, almost in sympathy. "Not to worry, guv. I'm used to people laughing at me.

"Now then, the team don't seem hurt. Mayhap they were just frightened-like. And the chaise don't seem damaged, either."

The marquess could hardly believe the docile animals that stood so quietly without a single twitch were the frenzied pair of a few minutes ago. "You have a magic touch with horses, boy," he said admiringly, reaching into his pocket for his purse.

"No, that's all right, guv," the boy said, patting one of the team's necks. "You can pay me in London."

"In London?" Sinclair echoed.

"Why, sure. Your tiger ain't no good to you no more, and won't be for a long time. But I'll take his place, and we can be on our way as soon as you've spoken to the doctor."

"But how can you come with me?" Sinclair asked. "What of your parents? Your master? And, come to think of it, what were you doing in the road like that, at this time of night?"

"I couldn't sleep, sir," the urchin said, his eyes all limpid blue sincerity. "I was out taking a little walk. And I'm sorry for your trouble. Least I can do is help you get to town. And don't you worry about me. My parents, well, I don't know where they might be. I can't even remember them. And I don't have a master. Not yet, at any rate, I don't," he added, peeking up at the stern face of the marquess with a little grin.

The arrival of the doctor forestalled any reply Nick Sinclair might have made, although he promised himself he would pursue the matter when he had more time.

Half an hour later, he left the inn. Henry's foot had only been badly bruised, not crushed as his master had feared, but there was no way he would be able to stand on it for some time. The marquess left money with the innkeeper for the lad's care, and that man's wife promised she would do her best to restore him to health. Flushed with crying, and only now in less pain from a dose of laudanum, Henry stammered his thanks.

Sinclair made his escape. If the redheaded urchin was still game, he would be on his way again. Even with the delay, he could make London before the moon set.

The boy stood by the horses' heads, and he bowed a little when he saw the marquess approaching.

"Ready to leave, guv?" he asked.

Sinclair thought him a bold lad. He was used to obsequious, well-mannered servants who only spoke when asked a direct question. But somehow he could not put this boy in his place with a few cutting words. It was as if he knew he meant no disrespect—that it was his way to be outspoken.

"Yes, all has been taken care of. Now, are you sure you are free to go with me? I'll have no furious master baying at my heels after his indentured servant, will I? And be sure you tell me the truth. I have a short way with liars."

"No problem, guv. Free as the breeze, I am," the boy said with another cheeky grin. He waited until the marquess was settled in his place and had hold of the reins before he moved to the perch at the back.

"Hang on tight," Sinclair said curtly over his shoulder. "I want no more accidents this night."

No words were exchanged by the two as they traveled toward the metropolis. The marquess was brooding about the vast amount of money he had wagered—and lost—at that afternoon's bout. He wondered why that should be so as he slowed the team for the steep hill he could see ahead. He never wasted any time in regret. No, his custom was to wager on a whim, and if he lost, pay his debt and walk away. He behaved much the same when he won. Money was, after all, only money.

But now, his man of business's words at their last meeting came vividly to mind as well. "I do assure you, m'lord, I do not speak without reason," Abner Barrett had said. "Nor do I raise a false alarm. That is far from the case. I mention this only because if your lordship continues as he has been doing, he will have no fortune left. We will be forced to mortgages, land sales—selling other assets. All most ill-advised, for once gone, such things can rarely be recovered."

Nicholas Sinclair had scoffed and called Barrett an old woman. But although the man had flushed, he had not backed down. Idly, the marquess wondered if it were possible he could be in such a bad case. Then he snorted. For as long as he could remember, he had possessed vast wealth. His numerous estates were profitable, his investments sound. Barrett was a good steward, and a careful one. He himself had always thought he had so much money he need not consider it; indeed, he did not believe he had to practice frugality like some little clerk, even now. Was he not the Marquess of Rockford? And what, after all, did he spend money on? He had no expensive wife to dress and frank and indulge, and he spent nothing on his various homes except for occasional repairs. Not for him the new gilded furniture, expensive porcelain, silver, and art. No, all he did was buy horseflesh when he fancied it, keep himself decently clothed, and wager, as all gentlemen did. Well, there were his carriages as well, but surely they were a mere bagatelle. And his mistresses, of course. He admitted they were costly.

A picture of the enormous number of servants who occupied all his establishments far and wide flashed through his mind and he shrugged. It was true, most of them were idle a great deal, but when he decided to visit one of his country places, he expected everything to be running as smoothly as if he had spent the entire year there. A man must live, after all. And surely his position dictated that he live graciously.

Barrett must have exaggerated! Besides, he had no intention of giving up his card games—all his play. It was the one thing that seemed to amuse him these days. Then a little smile lifted one corner of his mouth as the chaise reached the top of a hill and he could see in the distance the red glow in the sky that hung over London's streets. He had been in error. Wagering was not the only thing. There was Lucy as well.

When he pulled up before his mansion on Park Lane, he did not have to give an order, for almost before the team came to a halt, the redhead was off his perch and running. Sinclair admired his speed, although he knew there was no need for it. The team was too tired to act up after the long day.

"The stable is in the mews behind," he said brusquely as he tossed the reins aside and climbed down. "Can you see to the team yourself?"

"Sure thing, guv," the lad said.

"You'd better bed down in the loft there. My head

groom's name is Finn. Tell him who you are in the morning. He'll see you get breakfast and some clothes more suitable to your station.

"That reminds me, you've yet to tell me your name."

"Didn't ask, did you?" the boy retorted with his gap-toothed grin. "I'm called Toby, I am."

Impatient, the marquess nodded and began to walk away.

"Does this mean I'm your new tiger, guv?" the boy called after him softly.

Nicholas Sinclair waved a careless hand, and Toby chuckled to himself as he led the weary team away.

London streets were not the safest place in the world late at night, but the marquess had never worried about that. Besides, it was almost dawn. Few people were abroad. He supposed even the dregs of London had to sleep sometime.

It took him fifteen minutes of rapid walking to reach the little house where he had installed his mistress. He did not knock. He had a key. There was enough light coming through the front parlor window for him to make out the dark bulk of the stairs, and he took them easily, two at a time, making no effort to be quiet. Lucy's door was closed. He pushed it open and stepped inside.

"You'd better be m'lord Rockford," a little soprano said coolly. "If you're not, you're a dead man."

He laughed and moved to the dressing table to light the candle there. As soon as she heard his voice, Lucy laughed with him and put down the pistol she had been clutching in both hands.

In the flickering candlelight, Nicholas Sinclair admired the lavender nightrobe she was wearing. It was nothing but a wisp of lace and gauze. She might as well have been naked. Indeed, he had bought it for her for that reason. She threw back the satin spread that covered her and sank back on her pillows, raising her arms over her head to stretch.

The marquess shrugged out of his coat and tore off his cravat. Lucy watched him, a little smile on her face. She looked for all the world like a kitten who had been given an unexpected saucer of cream. She did like this one, she told herself. He wasn't cruel, and he treated her well. Besides, he was clean and handsome, too.

As she opened her arms to him, Lucy hoped he would not tire of her for a very long time.

Two

Two weeks later, Toby had settled down to the routine demanded of the Marquess of Rockford's tiger. He had only to be instantly available, no matter the hour of day or night, when the marquess wished to drive out. Once they had gone on an overnight trip to a certain viscount's estate near Reading. Play had been heavy, or so Toby heard from the viscount's servants. From the glum looks of the other gentlemen in the party the following day, and the easy air Nick Sinclair sported, it was plain that this time he had won handily.

Perhaps that was why he had tossed his tiger a guinea when they reached London again, or perhaps it was just to see his gap-toothed grin. Who could tell? Toby had heard what his master's friends thought of him, for they seldom bothered to lower their voices in front of servants. He had been called an "unpleasant little beggar," a "brash bounder," and a "bran-faced monkey." The marquess never bothered to defend his choice, but neither did he look about for a replacement. Although no words passed between the two, Toby knew he had been accepted.

This particular morning, however, the tiger was nowhere in evidence. Sinclair was walking on Bond

Street with an acquaintance of his named Bartholomew Whitaker whom he had met by chance.

"Going to Brighton this summer, Rockford?" Whitaker inquired, bowing to the Countess of Wills, who was passing in an open landau. The countess favored them both with a charming smile.

"I've not decided," the marquess said absently. "Can't say I find it that enthralling. Just consider Prinny and his ghastly palace, those deadly receptions he insists on giving, the heat of the rooms and his interminable concerts. No, perhaps I'll try some other watering place this year. Something, mm, more out of the way."

Bart Whitaker's long thin face struggled mightily to contain a smile. All the men in the ton knew of the marquess's new mistress, and most of the ladies as well.

Suddenly Whitaker stopped and removed his top hat to bow to a girl who was approaching them, followed by her maid. Idly, Sinclair wondered who she was. He could not recall her face, and surely he would have remembered it if he had ever seen it before, as animated and lovely as it was. Under the lady's smart sea-green bonnet, her dark hair gleamed like black satin, and the light pelisse she was wearing could not hide her excellent figure. But as she drew nearer, it was her eyes that held his attention. They were a very clear, very pure green, framed in dark curling lashes.

"Why, Bart!" she exclaimed, holding out both her hands. As he took them and drew her close to give her a hearty kiss, he said, "So you have come to London at last, have you, Tory? You make me feel ancient! Surely it was not that long ago that I dandled you on my knee."

She laughed, and several people passing by

turned to look at her. The marquess did not wonder at it. Her laughter was pure music.

"You never did such a thing, and you know it," she scolded lightly. "Papa would have had your head if you had ever tried, for you know there are not that many years between us, sir. I fear I make a most elderly debutante."

"Surely not," Whitaker protested while his companion wondered at the lady's openness.

"I am twenty-one now, Bart. Compared to the young things of seventeen and eighteen, I'm practically on the shelf."

As she laughed again, the marquess coughed. He could not like being ignored.

Whitaker begged his pardon at once, explaining he had forgotten his manners in the joy of seeing this particular friend again. Turning to her, he added, "Allow me to present Nicholas Sinclair, Marquess of Rockford, my dear. M'lord, Miss Victoria Emerson."

As she held out her hand, the marquess took it and held it in his own. "Delighted, Miss Emerson," he said, never taking his eyes from her face. "I do assure you that you are a long way from being on the shelf. Indeed, I predict you will take society by storm this season."

Her eyes widened at his boldness, and he turned smoothly to his companion and added, "I'm sure you agree with me, don't you Whitaker? Tell Miss Emerson she may be easy. I give no idle compliments."

"No, you don't. But I'm positive Tory knows full well the devastating effect she has on our sex."

"I don't think I should be encouraging this very improper conversation. I am sure it is not at all the thing," she said, shaking her head at both men.

Sinclair saw her color was a little heightened, but he also noted she was not in the least disconcerted. A point for Miss Emerson.

"I take it I may assume, since you are in town, that your father did not approve the latest aspirant for your hand, Tory?"

Behind Miss Emerson, her maid stood stolidly waiting, although Nick Sinclair could see she was listening to every word. Was she more than a maid perhaps? Some sort of companion, or chaperon?

"How do you know these things, Bart?" the lady asked tartly. "You have not been home to the country in months!"

"Oh, I manage to keep informed, even if I am not on the scene. I did not think poor Frank had a chance with you, but how was I to tell the boy? It was obvious he was smitten at Christmas."

"You are very bad, and I have no intention of discussing it. Besides, I must be going. Mama will be wondering what is keeping me.

"So nice to have met you, m'lord Rockford. Bart. Come along, Essie."

With a final, delicious smile, she left them, and Whitaker chuckled as soon as she was out of earshot.

"What a little beauty," the marquess remarked as they set out again in the opposite direction. "I don't wonder she has an army of beaux."

"Oh, Tory is a pearl without price. One hopes her father will relent one of these days and allow her to wed."

"But how can this be?" the marquess asked, intrigued. "Generally fathers cannot wait to get their daughters off their hands."

"Mr. Emerson is the exception that proves the rule, then. Tory is his only child, and he has refused at least four offers that I know of for her hand. There may well have been more."

"Four? What do you suppose he is looking for? Or were they all poor, ill-connected unfortunates?"

"No, indeed. If I were to mention names, you would be astounded. But perhaps it is just as well he is so particular. Tory has never seemed to care a snap of her fingers for any male. I shall be interested to see the gentleman she finally chooses. Yes, indeed."

"Perhaps you will be the one," the marquess said idly. He had lost interest in the conversation for the shop window they were just passing contained a lovely pearl pendant on a long silver chain. He wondered how it would look around Lucy's neck. The chain was long enough so the pendant would rest between her full, high breasts.

Bartholomew Whitaker's snort recalled him to present company.

"Not I," he said. "We are neighbors in the country. Why, I have known Tory since she was a little girl. It would be like marrying my sister."

At the corner the marquess took a courteous leave of the gentleman, and forgot all about him and the handsome Miss Emerson as he retraced his steps to the jeweler's shop.

He spent the afternoon at White's playing cards, and again his luck was definitely in. It was such a novel experience for him that he wondered at it. It was almost as if he could not lose. Not that he won every hand, of course. Still, when he rose hours later, he was certainly plump in the pocket.

"Never saw such a streak of luck in all my born days," Randolph Sperling muttered, running a hand through his Brutus crop. He had lost heavily and steadily all afternoon, and he sounded truculent.

"Play and pay, Randy, old son. Play and pay," Marmaduke Ainsworth said with a wicked grin. "Have to agree, though. Nick's luck has surely turned."

"I don't understand it myself," that gentleman admitted as he pocketed his winnings and the vowels Sperling had written for him toward the end. "I must say it makes a nice change. You do remember my wretched hands in the past? It would be better if you were to rejoice in my good fortune now, instead of complaining."

"And so we might, if we were only watching you fleece others," Kit Lawson, the fourth person at the table said lightly. "I'm off tomorrow, and just as well after this day's work. My father has summoned me home, no doubt to ring a peal over me. I'll probably stay and rusticate for a while. I doubt he'll advance me anything till quarter day."

"Going to tell him about today?" Ainsworth inquired.

Nick shuddered and shook his head, and Ainsworth laughed.

Nicholas Sinclair walked home alone through the warm golden afternoon. He decided to order the chaise—take a drive. He had no dinner engagement, and only a few casual commitments for that evening. He had said he might look in at the Duchess of Norwood's soiree, and he had half agreed to meet friends later to investigate the latest hell. But although in the past that would have been first on his list of priorities, today it didn't seem to hold much appeal. Perhaps because he had already spent the afternoon at play, and won so handily?

23

Besides, the hell wasn't going anywhere. He was sure its proprietess, a Mrs. Tandy, would be delighted to welcome him whenever he showed up. He chuckled lazily as he wondered if his new streak of luck would hold. It would be a shame to break the lady's brand-new bank. Just as well he had decided not to bother tonight.

At home in Park Lane, he ordered the chaise brought around. Minutes later, as he came down the steps pulling on a tight pair of leather driving gloves, his new tiger stood at the team's heads, giving him his usual cheeky grin.

Once again, the marquess marveled at the ease with which the lad controlled the highbred team. He thought he looked much better in his dark green livery with the brass trim and buttons, although with that flaming mop of hair and his round, freckled face, who would notice his clothes?

"I have 'em," he said brusquely as he picked up the reins. Toby swung up behind as the marquess gave the team the office to start. Nothing was said until they had passed through the outskirt villages, and the team settled down to a mile-eating canter.

"Going to Richmond, guv?" Toby inquired.

His master nodded.

"Nice afternoon for a drive, ain't it?" the tiger persisted. "The team will be glad of the exercise. That little jaunt through the park yesterday hardly broke a sweat on 'em."

"I know. But one does not tear through Hyde Park. It simply isn't done."

" 'Course not. I know *that*. Ain't stupid, you know," Toby said stoutly.

"I don't know why I put up with you," the marquess remarked, as if to himself. "You're not a handsome addition to the ranks of my servants, you've got an impertinent tongue on you, you don't know your place, and you get into fights. Yes, I heard about that fracas in the stable. Finn told me you went for Jemmy with both fists flying."

"He was deliberately hurting the stable cat, guv. I can't abide to see an animal abused, I can't."

"You must have some science the rest of us have not acquired. Jemmy has at least twenty pounds on you, and he's taller as well. How did you manage to best him?"

"I surprised him," Toby said after a little pause. "And I was in the right."

"Don't do it again," the marquess said coldly.

"I won't need to," Toby was quick to say. "Jemmy's learned his lesson."

The marquess refused to be drawn, and the rest of the drive to Richmond was accomplished in silence. After a quick stop at a pub there for a pint of ale, he returned to town.

"I trust the sweat the team has broken is to your satisfaction, sir?" the marquess inquired a little sarcastically as he climbed down in Park Lane.

Toby only grinned. "They'll do fine, guv. Will you be needing me anymore today?"

"Why do you ask?"

"I thought I'd go and see the sights," the tiger confided.

The marquess gave his permission, only warning him to be careful before he waved a dismissal, and Toby, whistling a cheerful tune, led the team away to the mews.

After a solitary dinner, Nicholas Sinclair decided to attend the duchess's soiree, at least for a short time. He had the pearl pendant in his pocket. He would take it to Lucy later, he decided, looking forward to the way she would show her gratitude.

It was quite late before he made his appearance at the Norwood's town house in Portman Square, and the receiving line had long since dispersed. He gave his hat and walking stick to a footman who bore them reverently away before he mounted the stairs, nodding to those he met. Inside the largest drawing room, he accepted a glass of champagne from a footman's tray and looked about him. It was only April, but the room was crowded. The duchess must be in alt, he thought as he sipped his wine. But perhaps there was wisdom in giving an early party. There was less chance that people would arrive bored, or at odds with each other, as so often happened at the end of the Season. But now they had only arrived in town and had much to discuss about their winter activities, and fresh gossip to exchange with their friends.

Marmaduke Ainsworth came up to talk about the afternoon's card game again. "Think Sperling's in the suds, Nick?" he asked. "Never saw the man so blue-deviled as he was today, and all because the cards didn't fall for him."

Sinclair shrugged. "I've no idea. But as you said, if he can't pay, he shouldn't play. I've no patience with a man who whines and complains at his luck."

"I say, why on earth is Gerald Emerson glaring at you? No, don't look yet. All right. He's speaking to Lady Jersey now."

The marquess turned to see a middle-aged man bowing to the talkative lady who was known as "Silence." He was gray-haired and a little overweight, something his well-tailored evening clothes could not entirely disguise. As he watched, the gentleman turned back and their eyes met. Nicholas Sinclair bowed slightly. Mr. Emerson, if that was who he was indeed, turned very red, stiffened, and abruptly about-faced.

"Singular," Ainsworth murmured at the marquess's elbow. "Been taking *his* money at cards, too?"

"I've never met the man."

"But, then, why . . . ?"

"I imagine because he's learned I was introduced to his beauteous daughter this morning. I suspected that maid she had with her was more than just a servant. It is obvious I am being warned away from the lady, wouldn't you say? How lowering for me, to be judged so quickly and found wanting."

"Man must be an idiot. Every mother in the ton has been after you for years."

"Even though I'm a rake and a gambler? A thoroughly bad risk? Or so I have heard it whispered."

"*That* wouldn't matter to most of 'em. It's the title and wealth they want, and it's my opinion you'd have to be an ax murderer before they'd look at you askance.

"No, no, don't look so fierce at *me*. Only telling you what's what. Not that you don't know it already, so courted and petted as you are. But there are others, y'know. Don't believe you're as bad as you've been painted. Or maybe they think you can be redeemed by the love of a good woman."

The marquess snorted, and Duke Ainsworth grinned. "I know, old chap, but it's the silly sort of thing women do believe. My own mother must be one of 'em, for she was mentioning you only a few weeks ago. She's bringing out another one of my cousins this season. But don't worry. The mater took one look at the little dear and lowered her expectations. Wispy, witless, and, er—spots."

Nick Sinclair wisely refused to comment on the unfortunate young lady. But as Ainsworth watched, a light began to glow deep in his gray eyes, and his well-sculpted mouth curved in a little smile.

Somehow it was not a pleasant smile, and Ainsworth hastened to say, "Nothing amusing about it. Assure you we'll be lucky to fire the gel off at all. And I'm the one who has to squire her about, worst luck."

Sinclair said he had been thinking about something else, and the two parted. For a while, the marquess studied the throng passing to and fro before him. At last, as that throng parted momentarily, he caught a glimpse of Victoria Emerson across the room. She was talking to a pair of attentive gentlemen, and the marquess straightened up from the wall that had been supporting his shoulders, and began to make his way to her side.

The wild plan he had conceived while speaking to Duke Ainsworth had returned full force. So, Mr. Gerald Emerson did not want the Marquess of Rockford anywhere near his precious daughter, did he? In that case, how very amusing it would be to make a dead set at the girl, treating her to a desperate flirtation before he abandoned her. He admitted that what he planned to do was not the act of a gentleman. But hadn't this Mr. Emerson— whoever *he* might be—already decided he was not one?

Nicholas Sinclair felt entirely vindicated in this case. Besides, Bart Whitaker had told him the girl cared nothing for her beaux. His plan would not break *her* heart. But the ensuing alarm and apprehension such a mad courting would cause her fond papa would more than repay him for daring to snub—yes, *snub!*—Nicholas Sinclair.

What Ainsworth had said about him had been no surprise. He was sure there were those in society who warned their daughters, even their sons, to have nothing to do with him. But not a one of them had ever ventured to turn his or her back on him before. No one.

And that, the marquess told himself coldly as he elbowed a fat old gent aside, was something he had no intention of letting go unpunished.

Three

*H*E HAD LITTLE trouble ousting the gentlemen who formed Miss Emerson's court, and after he seated her, he beckoned to a footman to bring them both champagne.

"Neatly done, sir," she said, sounding amused.

"Getting you refreshment, ma'am?" he inquired innocently.

She chuckled. "Certainly not, as well you know. Poor Lord Quentin and Sir Donald! I imagine neither is quite sure how it happened that they found themselves dismissed."

"All they had to do was remain," he murmured, leaning closer. "I would have, in their place."

She considered him gravely, and she did not recoil. Sinclair told himself his plan promised to be even more entertaining than he had imagined.

"Perhaps they did not dare," she said at last. "There is something about you, sir, that is somewhat alarming. An air of barely leashed emotion, perhaps. Or do you think me fanciful?"

"Entirely. I have excellent control over my passions. I will, however, admit that where you are concerned, I am intrigued. I do not think I have ever seen a lady like you."

She waved a dismissing hand. "Then, I don't

imagine you have looked very hard. I am in no way unusual."

"I beg to differ," the marquess said as he rose from the sofa they were sharing. An older lady who looked somewhat like Miss Emerson was approaching, with a young gentleman close behind. He had no intention of sharing his prize with her mama and others.

"You are unique," he added, holding her eyes with his own. "You have a great deal of conversation, a lively wit, and a welcome poise. And your beauty is most compelling. No, you must not argue the point, ma'am! Trust me. You *are* unique."

He bowed to a suddenly speechless Miss Emerson, and smiled before he moved away. Behind him, he heard the lady's mother ask who he was, and he smiled more broadly. He must go carefully, although he did not think the Emersons would go so far as to insist their daughter give him the cut direct. As an only child, she was probably much indulged, and, of course, she had never shown any indication she had ever been attracted to any of her suitors. But best he only woo her desperately when her parents were not nearby, or that dragon of a maid of hers.

And when would that be, and where? he wondered as he bid the duchess good-bye and thanked her for a pleasant evening.

"Evening, my left foot," the elderly lady said tartly as she adjusted her slipping stole. "You've been here less than an hour or so, you naughty Nicky! I'm sure you're off someplace most unsuitable, and thank you, I don't care to hear a word about it. I'm fond of your Aunt Martha, and what I don't know, I can't be forced to divulge."

He laughed at her and bent to give her a kiss before he ran down the stairs. The Duchess of

Norwood sighed as she watched him, all broad shoulders and taut muscles under his black evening clothes. The light from the chandelier above him made his dark head gleam. He looked up and caught her watching him as a footman brought him his hat and cane, and he blew her another kiss.

The duchess smiled, even as she told herself it was too bad, the path he had taken through life. Still, she admitted she had always had a soft spot for rakes and renegades, although such a thing was hardly to her credit. But as she turned back to her guests, she reminded herself that worthy people could sometimes be so boring. And pinning on a patient smile as she saw Maud Keating approaching, she amended that to deadly.

Miss Victoria Emerson certainly would have agreed with her that Lord Rockford was a fascinating man. As she smiled and conversed, she told herself she must be sure to ask Bart Whitaker about him. He was almost too bold. And there was something about him that both attracted and repelled her. There were many men here more handsome by far, but his strong features and determined jaw must always command attention.

And he certainly had a smooth way about him! Those polished compliments, that admiring, rueful smile, the soaring height of a brow quirked in amusement—all these things drew her. Yet she sensed there was another side to him. A side darker than his hair, his brows. She was sure he could be ruthless, if he chose.

Her father had warned her about him this afternoon. Told her he was no better than he should be with his unfortunate reputation, his incessant gambling, his dwindling wealth. Told her the man had no concern at all for his good name, and was sullying it further every day. Warned her, in fact, to be on her guard with him.

Miss Emerson smiled now and agreed to join Viscount Dorr's walking party in Hyde Park the following afternoon. She had not heard a single thing the viscount had been saying to her, but she was sure she hadn't missed anything. She had discovered some time ago that it was only necessary to smile occasionally, nod in admiration, and agree wholeheartedly while she kept her own counsel, at least with most men. But never Rockford. No, not him.

Much later, on the drive home, she told her father of the people she had met and talked to. She did not, however, mention the Marquess of Rockford until her mother reminded her of him.

"To be sure, he did sit beside me briefly. As Essie told you, Papa, Bart Whitaker introduced me to him on Bond Street this morning. I do not think I care for the gentleman. He seems very full of himself, does he not?"

Mr. Emerson sat back on his leather seat in relief. He was riding facing back, and in the light of the two side candles in sconces, he had a good view of his daughter's face. He could detect no consciousness on her part. But, of course, he should have realized that his Tory had too much good sense to be taken in by a rogue! Still, he would warn Miss Essex to keep a sharp eye out for the man. Tory was so beautiful.

"Is it tomorrow morning you are promised to Cousin Anne, my dear?" he asked his daughter. "I know you enjoy her company, but you must not let her impose on you. There will be a great number of demands on your time this spring, and I do not want you falling ill because you have undertaken

33

too much. Besides, Anne does not move in society anymore. I fear she has become a bluestocking, and therefore of no use to anyone."

"Darling Papa, how you do fret about me! I'm as hearty as a horse, and you know it. In fact, I have often thought how much more the delicate lady I could appear if I had only learned to faint occasionally."

The horrified exclamations of her parents made her laugh, relieved she had successfully diverted them from the subject of her visits to her older relative, visits she had no intention of abandoning. Living in the country, she had seen Anne only a few times. Now she was in London, she intended to see much more of her. Anne was intelligent, witty, charming, and educated. Tory Emerson loved her parents, but there was no denying they were not the most stimulating of companions. Her father fussed over her until sometimes she had to excuse herself lest she scream at him. And her mother, alas, was only a dear wigeon who looked to her husband not only for guidance, but for her ideas and opinions as well.

The next morning, Tory Emerson ate her breakfast in bed, as her father had suggested she do in town. She had derided the suggestion when it had first been made, but she had come to see its advantages. This way she could rise early, dress, and be on her way before anyone else in the family was up. And it meant she could take a footman with her, instead of her old governess, Matilda Essex. She was beginning to wish that lady would retire, or her father pension her off. She could not like the feeling she was being spied on, her every move reported back to Gerald Emerson.

Now, as she threw back the covers and padded to

the dressing room, Victoria Emerson shook her head a little. How silly Essie's supervision was when she was such an elderly debutante. That had been mostly her father's doing. Of course, there had been Grandmother Emerson's death when Tory was seventeen, the mourning of which put paid to that season, and her mother's ill health the following spring. And then her father had carefully explained to her his aversion to early marriage, before a girl was ready for it. He had made it sound quite perilous, and Tory had all she could do not to giggle at him. But, then, he meant well, and he did worry so about her! And to tell truth, she didn't seem to care about getting married. Sometimes she wondered if she might be abnormal.

Eventually Mr. Emerson had had to relent. He had a great deal of business to attend to here in town this year, so he had rented a house on South Audley Street. And he himself had taken his daughter to the best dressmakers, to make sure she had the most beautiful gowns and accessories. Both she and her mother were dumbfounded at the amount of money he had spent. It had been as if he, having capitulated at last, wanted his daughter to outshine all the rest. Tory had talked him out of a gala ball to mark her come-out, saying she had no desire for such a thing at her age. But she was sure the fact the house he had engaged had only the smallest of ballrooms was what had forced him to abandon the scheme.

That morning she was on her cousin's doorstep at the unfashionable hour of nine-thirty. She discovered the lady still at the breakfast table, and kissed her lightly before she took the seat across. A maid poured her coffee.

"You quite put me to shame," Anne Garen said as

she buttered another scone. "To think I am discovered languishing about here, instead of in a bustle with my morning chores. Alas, you have found out how indolent I am!"

Victoria Emerson laughed at her as she stirred cream into her coffee. Her cousin was ten years the elder, the only daughter of Mrs. Emerson's elder brother. She had been married once for a brief time. Her husband, Lord Garen, an amateur archaeologist, had been killed on an expedition to Egypt when she was only nineteen. Since that time, she had lived alone in London, much to the consternation of all her horrified relations. Anne Garen only smiled at them and went her own way, which was, she told an awed Tory Emerson, quite the best thing about being a widow.

She was a tall woman who tended to slump until she remembered her posture. Her face was pleasant; her best feature, her large, tip-tilted blue eyes. She disliked those eyes. She considered blue an insipid color, and the angle they were set in her face, catlike. Her hair, a soft nut brown, was not unusual. But there was something about her that drew people's attention. Perhaps her smile? Tory wondered as she sipped her coffee. Or was it her air of calm independence that made people ask who she was?

"Did you enjoy the Norwood do last evening?" Anne Garen asked, interrupting Tory's musings.

"Yes, I did. It's strange, you know. I never expected to like London society en masse, but I had a very pleasant time. Indeed, some of the people I met had a great deal of knowledge, wit, and common sense, and some were vastly amusing."

"I shall ask you if you feel the same about them in six weeks time," her cousin warned. "And if you say the same thing, I'll be amazed. I've discovered, as I'm sure you will, that these wonderful, witty, warm people never have anything new to contribute after first meeting. Except gossip."

"Is that why you stopped going about in the ton?" Tory asked.

"Do have a scone, dear. They're delicious. Yes, that was the reason. To be sure, I still see a few kindred spirits, but I avoid the usual balls and soirees, tea parties and breakfasts. In fact, I am seldom invited anywhere, for everyone knows I will refuse to attend. And it is not pleasant to have parties *you* consider to be the height of elegance and daring, scorned. I don't blame my erstwhile hostesses a bit for ignoring me."

"It would be fun if you were to come out with me sometime, though," Tory persisted.

"So I can see firsthand all the beaux you are attracting? I should be bored witless."

"I did not mean that at all, but I'll not rise to your bait. Tell me, Anne, do you know the Marquess of Rockford?"

Her cousin looked at her shrewdly for a moment. There had been something in Tory's voice—was the question asked too casually? Was Tory hiding something?

"Nicholas Sinclair? I have never met him, but I have heard of him, I think. Isn't he the one who is going to the devil with his wagers and play?"

"So they say. Bart Whitaker introduced us yesterday. And last night he sat with me, and we talked for a while."

"Did you like him?"

"I don't know. He can be charming. In fact, at the time I suspected he was trying to get up a flirtation with me. But that cannot be. I understand he avoids young ladies of good family."

"But not the others," her cousin said dryly.

Tory chuckled. "No. I wish you could have been there when Mama told me of his mistresses, Anne. She was scarlet with embarrassment, but no doubt Papa insisted.

"I wonder why the marquess was so attentive, though," she concluded.

Lady Garen looked at her across the breakfast table. Dressed in a new white muslin gown sprigged all over with dainty pink roses, and wearing matching pink kid gloves and sandals, with a white chipped straw bonnet decorated with more pink roses on her glossy black curls, Victoria Emerson was a picture. Whenever she walked out, she would be sure to stop everyone from dukes to dustmen in their tracks. And the best thing was, she did not even realize how lovely she was. Lady Garen chuckled to herself. What a miracle it was that the girl's doting father and mother had not succeeded in ruining her.

"Perhaps he did it for a wager?" she suggested as the two rose from the table.

"Why, I never thought of that. How horrid! I shall be decidedly cool to him if we should chance to meet again," Tory assured her.

Her cousin put an arm around her as they left the room. "Come, let us forget men, my dear. Tiresome creatures! I'll just run up and put on my bonnet, and we can be off. I am so anxious for you to see the Elgin Marbles. And then I have a surprise. I've made an appointment to visit a young artist's studio. He is not well-known as yet, but I think he will surprise everyone in a few years' time. His drawings are so fine, his oils so glowing. But you shall be the judge. Oh, do dismiss your footman, Tory. I'll see you home in my carriage later."

By the time Tory Emerson returned to South Audley Street, her parents were in a state of acute alarm. It was only one in the afternoon, but they acted as if she had been gone for days.

"But Papa, Mama, how can you take on so?" she finally demanded after her mother had wept tears of relief, and her father had scolded her fondly. "You knew I was with Cousin Anne."

"But why didn't you take Miss Essex? She is very hurt. And why did you dismiss the footman?" her father demanded.

"I do not like to spend every moment in Essie's company. And I was with *Anne*. There was no need for the footman to tag along, when we were in her carriage, attended by her coachman and groom. And my cousin delivered me right to the door, and waited until I was safely inside. My dears, I fear you are being gothic."

"It is just that we love you so," Mrs. Emerson wailed from behind her handkerchief.

Mr. Emerson had the grace to look a little ashamed, but still he launched into a long lecture on the evils of town. Tory ceased to listen.

She was studying a large bouquet of spring flowers that adorned the center table before the empty fireplace. There was a card beside it, one which, she was indignant to see, had been opened and read. Then she counted slowly to ten. It was her parents' right to read her correspondence, of course, even though she thought herself quite past the need for such interference. Still, she told herself, she must not take exception to it, lest they think the Marquess of Rockford meant something more to her than just a gentleman she had met casually.

Her father saw where she was looking, and added, "And that's another thing! Who are these whippersnappers who are sending you flowers on such a short acquaintance? I don't like it, Tory!"

"What whippersnappers?" she asked as she went to the table and calmly picked up the card. To her deep chagrin, the flowers were not from Nicholas Sinclair after all. They had been sent by Lord Quentin. Tory told herself the embarrassment and disappointment she felt was ridiculous.

"Were there other flowers?" she asked as she faced her parents again. "Somehow I was sure other gentlemen I met last evening would send some. Dear, dear, only one bouquet! I must not be as wonderful as you seem to think, my dears."

"But there was another, Victoria," her mother said, successfully diverted. "A posy of violets from Sir Donald. I had it taken to your room."

"I shall go and admire it. Are you coming with me to the modiste's this afternoon, Mama? I have a fitting on my silver and white ball gown."

"Oh, dear. I did not realize you needed me, Victoria. I'm promised to an old friend who is giving a loo party this afternoon. Of course I shall cancel immediately."

"No, no, there's no need. I'll take Essie with me. It will make up for my deserting her this morning. And then there's Viscount Dorr's walking party in Hyde Park. And is it tonight you are taking us to the theater, Papa? How busy we shall be, to be sure! Gay to dissipation in fact."

With a little laugh she was gone, running lightly up the stairs to the sanctuary of her room. As she went along the upper hall, she heard her father speaking to the butler, and she shook her head. Mama was one thing, she told herself, so easily outwitted and reassured. But her father was quite another. Yet somehow she had to find a way to make him feel easy, one that still afforded her a bit of necessary freedom. She felt as precariously balanced as the slack rope performer she had seen at a country fair once, but she knew it must be done.

Four

MUCH LATER WHEN the party of eight assembled in Hyde Park, Miss Emerson was delighted to see the viscount had included Bart Whitaker. At first she was forced to accept her eager host's arm, but eventually when the group changed partners, she found herself with her old friend.

"Are you finding our amusements tame after country life, Tory?" he inquired, smiling down at her. "You were never one for dawdling; as I recall, why, I seem to remember walks where I was challenged to keep up with you."

"Ah, but walking in the country and in town are two entirely different things. In the country one walks to get from place to place. Here, it is done to show oneself off."

"I can't believe you have become jaded after such a short time," he marveled.

"But I haven't," she insisted. "I'm enjoying myself immensely. So many new people to meet, so many fascinating things to do. Why, this morning I . . ."

She hesitated for a moment, then went on smoothly, ". . . Saw the Elgin Marbles. Have you had the opportunity? They are so powerful."

Bart Whitaker answered easily, but he had noticed that little hesitation, just as he had noticed the Marquess of Rockford's chaise sailing by at a

42

spanking pace. Rockford had had the lovely blond Countess of Wills up beside him. He wondered if that was the reason Tory had faltered, and he grinned to himself. This promised to become amusing.

Beside him, Victoria Emerson quietly seethed. She was furious with herself for her slip, and she hoped Bart had not noticed it. But now she could not ask him about the marquess, as she longed to do.

"I noticed you and Nick Sinclair in a tête-à-tête last evening at the Norwood soiree," he said, leaving Victoria to wonder if he could read her mind. "Do you like him?"

"He seems pleasant enough, but then, so are many others," she replied. "Have you known him well, Bart?"

To her surprise her friend paused, frowning. "Why, do you know, I don't think I do. Oh, of course I have known him ever since he came to town when he gained his majority, but I don't think I know him *well*. Strange, that. I would have thought I'd say he was a friend of mine. But I don't think he *has* any."

"But he seems to know everybody," she protested.

"Yes, and they know him. Superficially that is. But he doesn't let anyone get close to him. You are allowed to come just so far before he shuts some sort of invisible door in your face. Now, why has that never occurred to me before?"

"If it is true, I wonder why he does that?" Victoria asked, intrigued. "Everyone needs friends."

Whitaker had no time to comment, for just then the marquess's chaise appeared again. This time he was alone except for his tiger. The lad gave Tory a grin she would have considered insolent in another servant. Somehow on the boy's homely, freckled face, it made her smile widely in return.

"Miss Emerson, well met. Whitaker. May I persuade you, ma'am, to take a turn around the park with me?" the marquess inquired.

Victoria stood staring up at him, seated so far above her. The sun was behind him, making it difficult to read his face. That same sun turned the tiger's unruly red curls to a halo of flame.

"No, you may not, sir," she said, delighted to have this opportunity to depress his superiority. "I am with Viscount Dorr's party this afternoon."

The marquess saw that gentleman hurrying back, as if to make sure he did not lose Miss Emerson's company.

"Rockford," he said in his pleasant tenor. "Miss Emerson, Whitaker, the others are waiting for you to join them for an alfresco tea beside the Serpentine. Er, you're welcome to come as well, m'lord," he added.

His voice had been so devoid of animation as he extended the invitation that Tory could not look at either the marquess or Bart lest she dissolve in laughter.

"Kind of you, Dorr, but better not," Nick Sinclair said easily. "The team is still fresh.

"Give you good afternoon, ma'am. Gentlemen."

He tipped his hat to them before he drove away, the tiger clinging like a limpet to the perch behind. Victoria was startled to feel the slight pressure of Bart's hand over hers where it rested on his arm. She had not realized she was staring after the marquess as if mesmerized. As she began to walk again, she smiled at both her companions, determined to put the disturbing Nicholas Sinclair from her mind once and for all.

Some distance away, Toby leaned forward a little and said, "She's a nice lady, guv. Real pretty, too. Do you like her, then?"

Rockford preserved a dignified silence. He had given the boy much too much freedom, and look what he had got in return. Insolence. Presumption. Brassy gall. He had no intention of discussing Miss Emerson, indeed, any woman, with his tiger, and he intended to tell him so immediately. But remembering Toby's artless remark about the Countess of Wills after he had returned her to her friends, he could not help smiling a little. Toby had said the lady reminded him of a wet shirt. "You know how it sticks to you, guv?" he'd said. "And no matter how you try to pull it away from your skin, it comes right back? She's like that, that countess."

Now, emboldened when he saw one corner of his master's mouth curve in a smile, Toby went on, "It would be good if you did like her. And she seems like one who wouldn't bore you so quick."

"What on earth do you mean, bore me?" the marquess demanded. "Explain yourself!"

"I heard it from the other servants," Toby said. "They say you only keep a mistress for a bit. This Lucy you've got now—she must be something special. I 'spect she'll be gone soon, though."

"Silence!" the marquess roared in a voice so full of anger Toby quickly subsided.

"You keep a civil tongue in your head, boy, or *you'll* soon be gone!"

"Awright, guv," Toby said in a small voice.

They had reached the park gates now and turned onto Park Lane. As soon as the marquess got home, he quickly left the chaise and strode up the front steps without another word. One of his footmen, returning from an errand, paused and eyed the tiger.

"What's set *him* off, then?" he asked.

Implying he had no idea, Toby shrugged as he led the team away.

Nick Sinclair dismissed his butler with an angry wave of his hand, and shut himself up in the library. He was furious. He did not know why he had not dismissed Toby immediately. He stripped off his driving gloves and sailed his top hat onto a sofa before he poured himself a glass of canary. Settling down at his desk, he tried to control his hot temper.

After another glass of wine, he was more at ease. And then he remembered the lad's comment about the lady he had honored this afternoon, and he had to grin again. As he did so, he wondered how adorable, pampered Lady Wills would feel, being compared to a sopping wet shirt. Recalling how closely she had sat beside him in the chaise, her cloying perfume, and how she had leaned against him when he lifted her down to rejoin her friends, he had to admit Toby's description was apt.

In a better mood now, he went through the afternoon post.

He was promised to Randolph Sperling and some others that evening for dinner and cards. He had tried to refuse the engagement, but Sperling would have none of it, claiming that in honor, he could not refuse to play now, after he had won so brilliantly before. Sperling seemed determined to engage him in gambling as often as he could in a desperate attempt to regain the money he had already lost. From past experience, Nick Sinclair could have told him it was no use. When you needed money, you never won. Only when you didn't give a damn did the cards fall for you, the dice turn up the combination you needed, and your horse gallop home a winner by at least two lengths.

There were four men present that evening in Sperling's rooms in Jermyn Street. The dinner served by his man was adequate, the wines only tolerable. But, of course, none of those present had come for the cuisine or the drink. In almost indecent haste, the table was cleared, decanters of port and brandy set upon the sideboard, and new cards presented.

Leaning back in his chair, Nick Sinclair watched the others through narrowed eyes. Why had he never noticed how Hastings licked his lips in anticipation, and how his hands trembled? And how had George Gorham's nervous finger tapping as he sat on the edge of his seat escaped him before? Sperling especially was avid, although with his dark-ringed eyes and the little tic near one corner of his mouth, he did not look at all well.

Is that how I appear to people when I'm intent on gambling? Sinclair wondered idly as he cut the cards for deal. Surely not. These men seemed obsessed. And you aren't? something made him ask himself. Don't you remember how eagerly you've looked forward to a night of gambling? Who are *you* to criticize others?

Somehow this unpleasant picture of himself stayed with him as he picked up his hand, and he could not dispel it.

The evening dragged on as hand after hand was dealt. Hastings had donned the wide straw hat some gamblers wore, to hide their eyes and expressions when they sorted their cards. Gorham constantly mumbled under his breath to himself, and their host drank more than his share of brandy.

By two o'clock in the morning, Nick Sinclair rose from the table a substantial winner. The other three protested, saying it was not right he leave now.

"Why, the evening's still young, man," Gorham protested. "Here, let me pour you another glass of port. I feel my luck changing."

"I wish mine would," Sperling snarled, shuffling the deck with unsteady fingers. "I've lost more than I can pay. I'll—I'll have to ask for some time, Rockford."

There was a moment of awkward silence. In ton circles, gambling debts were paid immediately.

"Certainly," Sinclair said coolly. "Till quarter day, shall we say?"

"The devil take it," Hastings protested, tearing off his hat and throwing it on the floor. "Never saw such luck as you've had this evening, Rockford! It's not right or normal! Why, some might say there'd been dark doings here!"

The marquess put his hands flat on the table and leaned on them till his face was close to the man who had just spoken.

"Are you accusing me of cheating, sir?" he asked, his voice deceptively mild.

"Never said that, did I?" Hastings blustered, refusing to look Sinclair in the eye. "Just seems very strange to me, that's all. You win and win. You can't lose! When has that ever happened to anyone? Maybe the devil's got a hand in this."

"Now then, let us be calm, sirs," George Gorham interjected. He did not like the look on Nick Sinclair's dark face, or the deadly gleam in his eye. The tautness of his body reminded him of a drawn rapier. If care were not taken, he'd be forcing Hastings to retract his statement or asking him to name his seconds. "Yes, it is strange, I agree," he went on. "I've heard from others of your sudden, miraculous turn of luck, Rockford. Why, only last week, Duke Ainsworth swore you could not lose at dicing. And every cock you wagered on the following evening not only came up to scratch, but won its match. And that included a terrible long shot. Come now, sir, tell us how you do it."

To his relief, the marquess straightened and shrugged. "If I knew that, do you think I'd be likely to pass the knowledge around?" he asked. "I've no idea. It just suddenly seems I can't lose no matter what I wager on. Not all the time, of course. But often enough to remark. Perhaps I'll have to give up gambling."

He accepted his hat, gloves, and cane from Sperling's hovering manservant. "Do you know," he said, his hand on the doorknob, "although you probably won't believe me, it isn't anywhere near as fascinating when you *can't* lose. In fact, it gets downright tedious. Give you good evening, gentlemen."

Once on the street, Nicholas Sinclair paused for a moment to consider what he should do next. The mansion on Park Lane and the little house he had bought for his mistresses were equidistant. But somehow he had no desire to visit Lucy tonight. He had seen her yesterday afternoon, and although her lovemaking had been as expert and exciting as ever, she had annoyed him considerably. All the time he had been dressing, she had kept up a tedious monologue about a diamond bracelet she had seen at Rundell and Bridges. And he recalled that lately there was rarely a visit that did not end without her begging for something—jewelry, gowns, even her own carriage and pair. Sinclair knew he was a generous man, and Lucy more than well paid. It seemed that was not enough for her. He assumed most men, not just he himself, disliked being exploited. And yesterday Lucy had not so much wheedled and coaxed as she had demanded. Could it be she felt she had some power over him? He would stay away from her for a while, and then he would see.

As he turned toward Park Lane, he smiled grimly. *And* he had no intention of buying that damned bracelet. Enough was enough.

Avoiding the watchman who passed him calling out, "Two-thirty, a fair night, and all's well!" he went back over the evening he had just endured.

Strange he should think of it that way, he thought, brought up short by his choice of word. He had known those three men for years, and if they were not particular cronies of his, they were good fellows all. Well, most of the time.

He frowned now remembering Sperling's request for time before he paid his sizable debt. The man must be more done up than he had thought possible. Tonight, when he had seen he was not going to lose again, he had called a halt to the game, to spare his host.

Little good it had done! But from now on he would refuse to play with Sperling, although he doubted the man would ask him to until he had redeemed his vowels.

As he entered Berkeley Square, Sinclair recalled Hastings's accusation; how close to violence he had been. But what the man had said was true. He had no idea why he could not lose lately. He wished it had not happened, for he sensed people were talking about him, wondering. Oh, it had been all very well to recoup his heavy losses. Abner Barrett had been delighted with the change of events. But winning so much had taken all the joy out of wagering. Remembering how he had once looked forward so eagerly to a night of cards, a heavily contested horse race, even something as crazy as pitting two frogs against each other to see which could jump the farthest, made him feel bereft.

Ah, well, he thought as he turned down Mount Street, this can't last. Perhaps even by tomorrow this strange spell he was under would be gone. And good riddance, he told himself as he ran up his steps and sounded the knocker. His butler opened the door at once. Sinclair looked around the foyer. Two footmen stood against the wall. As was customary, no one would go to bed until he himself retired.

He was feeling hungry after the unappetizing dinner he had been served earlier, and he ordered supper brought to the library.

The butler bowed, his face impassive. But when his master was safely behind the closed library doors, he raised his eyes to heaven. The cook was not going to like the request at this hour, he told himself as he raised a finger to one of the footmen. Well, it couldn't be helped.

Over the delicious sliced chicken and his cook's special chutney, some salad and a basket of muffins, Nicholas Sinclair thought of Miss Victoria Emerson. He had seen how quick she had been to refuse his invitation to go around the park that afternoon. Still, he did not think she was indifferent to him. There had been a little spark in her eyes, a slight curve to her lips that were at odds with her crisp denial. He told himself he must find out more about her day's activities so he could intercept her at them. She probably slept late—most people in the ton did. But, of course, that was because they were often not in bed till dawn. Then the lady would either shop, visit friends, or attend various parties. He wished he could invite her to drive or walk openly, but he knew that was impossible in the face of her father's so obvious dislike.

Who did he know who could help him in his quest? he wondered as he buttered another muffin. He had thought of and discarded a score of society ladies, before he suddenly remembered Clarissa Carr. Lady Carr had been a close friend of his mother's, and she still professed a great fondness for him.

Surely she could be persuaded to give a garden fete, one that would include both he and Miss Victoria Emerson. She was fond of such entertainments, and the gardens surrounding her home near Richmond were outstanding. There was also the nearby Thames. Perhaps Miss Emerson could be persuaded to let him show her his prowess with the oars.

Feeling quite pleased with himself, and to the great delight of his servants, Lord Rockford took himself off to bed at last.

Five

A WEEK LATER Tory Emerson received an invitation to Lady Carr's afternoon party. A little perplexed, she showed it to her mother, for she could not recall ever meeting the lady.

To her surprise, her mother clapped her hands in delight. "Oh, my dear Victoria, how splendid, to be sure! Clarissa Carr, my word! Your father will be so pleased!"

"Why?" her daughter asked bluntly. "Who is Lady Carr?"

Mrs. Emerson's mouth worked helplessly for a moment, she was so shocked. "She is one of society's most revered hostesses, Victoria! We were both presented to the queen at the same drawing room when we were girls, although I am sure she does not remember *that*. But to be recognized by her is better than receiving a voucher to Almack's.

"Oh, what a coup it is! And sure to be outstanding. Lady Carr has always done things with great flair.

"I wonder where my invitation is?"

She rummaged through the pile before her on her desk, but nothing came to light.

"How very strange," she murmured at last. "Surely she does not expect you to go to the party without your mother in attendance."

"Mama, you are being gothic again. It is an afternoon party, to be held in a garden. There can be no impropriety in my going, perhaps with some other young lady."

Her mother looked doubtful. "I am sure Mr. Emerson will not countenance such a thing, and I beg you not to distress him by mentioning it, Victoria. Of course, it is a shame you must miss such a wonderful event, but your reputation and good name are more important than any festivity."

"And why is *my* reputation so fragile? Other much younger ladies are permitted a great deal more freedom than I am. And why should that be so?"

"Poor dears," her mother said simply. "Not to have Mr. Emerson for a father."

Tory excused herself and went to her room in a passion. Ringing for her maid, she began to get ready to leave the house. The knock on the door, followed by the entrance of a large, stern-looking woman tried her sorely.

"You are going out, Victoria?" Miss Essex said, sounding astonished. "You didn't tell me so. I must fetch my bonnet, my shawl."

"There is no need, Essie. I shall take a footman, for I am only going to my cousin, and I wish to be private with her."

The older woman stood stoically before her former charge, her hands folded as she gave her a disappointed look. "You spend too much time with Lady Anne. Your papa has often said so. It is not right. You should not go."

Tory had never gotten used to Matilda Essex's short way of speaking. She wondered if it was because she had been a governess for so many years, and had become used to instructing her charges in abbreviated form so they would be sure to understand her.

"Nevertheless, I am going. And I beg you will not try to detain me. I am not in very good temper this afternoon," Tory warned as she tied her bonnet on under her chin, then waved the tardy maid at the door away.

"Sit down. Tell me about it. I might help you."

"I cannot linger. Didn't I just say so? And Essie, you must remember there are many things I do not care to discuss with you, just as I am sure you have things you would not discuss with me."

"I do not. My life is an open book. Ask me anything."

Praying for patience, Tory fled.

When she arrived at her cousin's house a few minutes later, trailed by a stalwart footman, she was fortunate to find that lady within. Lady Garen took one look at her and went to pour them both a glass of sherry.

"Now, what has sent you up in the boughs, my dear?" she asked. "No, no, do not tell me yet! Sit down and take several deep breaths."

By the time Lady Garen handed her a brimming glass, Tory felt much calmer. "I do beg your pardon for bursting in on you this way, Anne," she said after a restorative sip. "It is just that I grow so impatient with Mama! And my father is not to be believed! Up to today I have managed to play a dutiful daughter, but Mama's saying I may not accept Lady Carr's invitation infuriated me. And do you know *why* I cannot go?"

"Because neither your father nor your mother were invited," her cousin said promptly.

"How did you know?" Tory demanded, amazed.

"Because that is the only reason in the world

that could make them insist you refuse. When Clarissa Carr gives one of her special fetes, all London clamors for an invitation."

"It isn't fair," Tory protested, looking mutinous. "Everyone will be there but me."

"Oh, you'll be there," Lady Garen said, getting up and going to the mirror where a few cards of invitation were stuck around the frame. Tory felt a sudden rush of hope when she saw Anne returning to her chair, holding the familiar invitation, and she leaned forward as the lady said, "I've also been asked, to my surprise. Of course, I did not intend to waste an afternoon in useless frivolity, but since I see you will fall into a green melancholy if you do not go, best I put my own wishes aside."

As Tory jumped up to hug her, she added, "But you must not make a practice of asking me to go about, now. This must be an exception."

"Oh, no, I won't," Tory promised. "Tell me, Anne, what do you make of Lady Carr's request that all the ladies wear white?"

"I am sure she has something planned. Or perhaps it is that she does not want her guests to overshadow her gardens. She is very proud of them, as well she should be. They are filled with the most beautiful flowers. And although it is early in the season, you are sure to be stunned by the display."

The two discussed the coming affair for some time. Lady Garen was even able to make Tory gurgle with laughter when she remarked that she was sure Mr. Emerson would insist his daughter travel in his own carriage, with at least two grooms as well as his coachman in attendance. She said she only prayed he would not feel the necessity for armed outriders as well.

That evening at dinner, Mr. Emerson was duly

informed of the flattering invitation his daughter had received. When he was told Lady Garen would be willing to chaperon Victoria, he gave his grudging consent. It was not what he liked, allowing his darling to gad about without him or her mother, no, not at all, but there was nothing he could do about it. And his wife had told him earlier that such invitations were not to be treated lightly, for this affair would establish their daughter as one of the foremost debutantes. Since Gerald Emerson had always considered her the undisputed leader of them, this would not have had much power to sway him, but when his wife whispered that she feared dear Victoria would be terribly disappointed if she were not allowed to go, he capitulated.

Only Mrs. Emerson was escorting her daughter to a ball that evening, to be given by Lord and Lady Handley. Gerald Emerson had intended to go as well, but the rheumatism that sometimes affected his lower back was bothering him, and he had been forced to plan an early bedtime. He hoped Mary would keep her wits about her. Sometimes, as he knew only too well, she forgot her duty in her enjoyment of the evening.

The two ladies kissed him good night and left in swirls of silk, and he went slowly up to his room on the footman's arm.

Almost everyone who was anyone had now returned to town, and the Handley ball was more than well-attended, it was so crowded that it made it unpleasant to try to get from one room to another.

Victoria Emerson was immediately claimed for the opening set of dances, and her mother, delighted to join a group of her particular friends, forgot all about her.

Much later, Victoria decided she must have a respite. She had danced almost continually, and the rooms were very warm from the heat of the scores of candles in the chandeliers and wall sconces. The number of people present and the unseasonable temperature also contributed to her discomfort. Even with the windows to the terrace open, it was still unbearable. She excused herself and made her slow way from the ballroom.

The Marquess of Rockford watched her go. He had spotted her earlier, and noticed the absence of her father, as well as the carelessness of her mother. Still, he had not approached her. He had decided to play a deep game with Miss Emerson, one that had involved leaving her to her own devices for a while. It had certainly worked with Lucy, he reminded himself with a grim smile. There was no reason it wouldn't work with the beauteous Miss Emerson as well. Women, good or bad—high or low—were much the same and almost always predictable.

But when she did not return for some time, he decided to seek her out. Of course, she could still be with a maid, repairing a ripped flounce or something, but he did not think that was where she had gone. He wasted little time on the major public rooms, jammed as they were with guests. Instead, he made his way to the back of the house. The door to Lady Handley's morning room stood open, and when he looked inside, he discovered Miss Emerson standing before an open window, fanning herself vigorously.

"You can easily catch cold doing that, after the heat of the ballroom," he told her as he came in, closing the door behind him.

Her eyes widened slightly, but she said nothing,

and she held her ground when he came much too close. Taking the delicate fan she held, he began to ply it gently before her face. Her complexion was rose-hued, and a few little curls had escaped her coiffure to cluster around her face. He thought them endearing, and scoffed at himself. But it was her scent that almost disarmed him, a scent made up of a light perfume and the essence of the girl herself. It was intoxicating.

She reached out suddenly and took the fan from him before she stepped back. "Thank you, m'lord, but I do not care for this kind of attention. And you should not have shut the door to the room when we are alone here. Be so good as to open it at once."

For a moment, she suspected he was about to refuse, even take her in his arms, and she held her breath until he bowed and went to do her bidding.

"Do you feel it safe enough now, ma'am, to be able to sit down and have a glass of wine with me?" he asked meekly.

Tory was not misled. The marquess was a dangerous man. Everyone said so. Still, she took the seat he indicated even as she wondered why she did not run away while she had the chance.

"This will make you feel more the thing," Rockford said as he handed her a glass of canary. "Devilishly hot, isn't it? I wonder you could dance every dance as you did, and not succumb to exhaustion earlier."

Tory almost asked how he knew that, but she suspected he was laying a trap for her. A trap she had no intention of falling into, she told herself grimly.

"Tell me, m'lord," she said instead, "Why are you so interested in me?"

His dark brows rose a little, but she did not look away from him, or lower her chin in confusion.

"You do not consider yourself a worthy object of adoration, Miss Emerson?" he asked, as if astounded. "I do assure you, you are thoroughly desirable."

"I am well-enough looking, I believe," she said easily. Going on before he could comment, she added, "But I have heard you have little or no interest in ladies."

One brow soared, and a light began to shine in his gray eyes. "You must tell me who told you such an untruth, ma'am. I've a score to settle with the gentleman," he said.

She could hear the amusement in his voice, and she felt a quick anger. "I did not say *all* women, sir," she told him stiffly. "I said *ladies*."

"So you did. Who has been talking to you about me? Spreading slander?"

"I do not think the truth can be considered slander, can it?" came the quick retort.

"And I must wonder why you engaged in such a conversation," he went on, as if she had not spoken. "Can it be you are, mmm, intrigued with me, ma'am? How very encouraging!"

Tory knew once again that her best course of action would be to rise now and take her leave, but she had no intention of behaving so sensibly. Besides, she had never been the sort of girl who abandoned questionable situations in simulated indignation. Now she made herself chuckle, and she was pleased to see some genuine astonishment cross Rockford's rugged face.

"How very conceited you sound, sir," she told him before she sipped her wine and set it on the table beside her. "Do forgive me if I damage your self-esteem a little. We have just recently met, and only spoken a few times. I know nothing of you. For all I do know, you might be the worst bore in London."

She held her breath as the silence that followed this pronouncement lengthened. At last he chuckled in turn and said, "Now, why do I suspect you would be quick to tell me I were, if it should turn out to be true?"

"I simply can't imagine," Tory said as she smoothed her gloves and rose. Slowly, he followed her example. "You must excuse me, now, sir. My mother will be wondering where I am."

As she curtsied, he said, "I doubt that. She is too enthralled with her friends. Shall you tell her about this tête-à-tête, I wonder? Regale her with our conversation on the drive home?"

Tory studied him coolly. The white of his linen was dazzling against his dark evening clothes, but it was his strong-featured face that drew the eye and held it.

"I rather doubt it," she said at last, making herself walk past him to the door. "I do not think she would find it that interesting. After all, what did it consist of? A few innuendos? Some sly remarks? Nothing of great import, at any rate."

Behind her, she heard him say, "That puts me in my place, doesn't it? Or at least you hope so. But *en guarde*, Miss Victoria Emerson. I am capable of making a quick recovery."

"I am said to have that ability myself. No doubt future meetings between us will be limited to verbal sparring. I am afraid that could become tedious."

She left him then, moving quickly down the corridor toward the sound of the music coming from the ballroom. But over that music, she imagined she heard his mocking laughter, and she could not for the life of her say who had won that encounter. Dare she hope she might call it a draw? she wondered.

On the drive home, her mother questioned her closely about her evening. Mary Emerson was feeling guilty for neglecting her daughter, and reminded that her husband would expect a full accounting on the morrow, memorized every name Tory volunteered. The Marquess of Rockford was not among their number. Instead, Mrs. Emerson heard all about Sir Angus McCree's breathless admiration, the clever things Viscount Dorr had said, how her old friend Bart Whitaker had taken her in to supper, and whom she had sat out with during the waltzes.

"Is it truly necessary for me to wait for approval before I waltz?" Tory asked finally, to divert her mother's attention from her beaux. "It does seem so silly when I am one and twenty."

"But you are just making your come-out, dear," her mother reminded her. "And better to be safe than sorry."

"Perhaps if you were to speak to one of the patronesses of Almack's, ma'am? Asked her to approve me?"

Mrs. Emerson threw up her hands and waxed eloquently about how ill-advised such a move would be. Tory stopped listening. Instead, she stared out at the dark streets and thought of Nicholas Sinclair, the Marquess of Rockford. The dangerous Rockford, she reminded herself. She wondered again why he was paying her so much attention. She found it impossible to believe he was falling in love with her. Not him! For unlike her other beaux, he was too smooth, too sophisticated for such a thing. Perhaps even too selfish? There had to be some ulterior motive for his behavior, but for the life of her she could not begin to imagine what it was. True, she was pretty, but so were many other girls. And although she would inherit all, the extent of her father's wealth was not likely to entice a gentleman of the marquess's stature. There were too many other girls of greater fortune, if his gambling debts were indeed as dreadful as she had been told. She did not even have a title.

And it was very strange, now that she thought of it. She had seen the marquess at almost every party she had attended, yet he had not singled her out before this evening. Once she had caught him watching her, but he had not asked her to dance, or even approached her, although he had honored several other ladies.

As the carriage halted and Tory Emerson prepared to get down, she shook her head. Rockford was the most inexplicable man she had ever met.

The man she was thinking about was even then making his way to the new hell, in company with Marmaduke Ainsworth. Earlier, Mr. Ainsworth had done his duty by his shrinking, wispy cousin, and now that she was safely restored to his mother, he was free to amuse himself.

"Tell me, Duke, have you heard any more of Sperling's affairs?" the marquess asked as they strolled along.

"Nothing at all. He's left town. Went the day after you took all his money, and everyone else's at the party."

"How did you learn of that?"

"Everyone knows. All over town," Ainsworth said. "Must warn you, Nick, there's been a storm of talk.

And Hastings, well, you know his wagging tongue. He says you've sold your soul to the devil. That nothing else could explain your phenomenal good luck."

Nick Sinclair looked grim. "Yes, he said much the same to me. I'm not in league with the devil, though, no matter what he claims. But I've noticed people are shying away from me. Wentworth had the temerity to refuse to play with me the other night. And Whitaker is another. Says even if he wanted to throw money away, he'd be damned if he'd throw any my way. I tell you, sir, it's getting unpleasant."

"Can imagine. Wouldn't care for it m'self."

"And it's not as if I know *why* my luck has changed, for I don't! But I'll tell you something. There's no fun in gambling when you can't lose."

His companion laughed. "Wouldn't mind finding *that* out for myself. The dibs haven't been in tune for me this age."

"Did you invite me to come hoping my luck would rub off on you?" the marquess demanded, sounding even colder than usual.

"Assure you, always enjoy your company, sir. But I'd be a liar if I denied it," came the easy reply. "Now, don't look black at me! Man must do what he can, especially when his luck turns fickle."

They had reached the discreet house where the new hell was located. The marquess noted the hired bruiser who paced up and down the street keeping watch. He'd be ready if uninvited guests tried to gain admittance. In addition, the door was opened cautiously in response to their knock, and a stout brass chain secured it. This Mrs. Tandy took no chances.

Ainsworth handed in his card of invitation.

"Brought someone with me, Fensen," he told the burly individual who peered at them suspiciously. "The Marquess of Rockford."

The doorkeeper, who had been in the act of slipping the chain stopped suddenly and shook his head. "Nah," he said. "Miz Tandy told me I wuz on no account ter let '*im* in."

Glancing quickly at the marquess, Ainsworth saw his cold glare, and he was quick to say, "Here now, what's all this about?"

" 'E's the gent wot's been winnin' everyone's money all over Lunnon, ain't 'e? Well, Miz Tandy sez 'e's not winnin' any '*ere*, an' that's final.

"Er—*ye* comin' in, Mr. Ainsworth?"

"Certainly not! Wouldn't think of it when you exclude my companion."

Suddenly Nick Sinclair went down the steps. "Don't be ridiculous, Duke," he said, his voice mocking. "There's no reason to be noble on my account, I assure you.

"I'll even wish you good fortune."

Before Ainsworth could reply, he had tipped his hat and was striding away, leaving the man to peer after him, confounded.

"Well, make up yer mind, do," Fensen chided as he threw the door wide. "Are ye comin' in, or ain't ye?"

Six

Nick Sinclair went to his mistress in a raging
temper. To think he had been turned from the door
of a common gambling hell, quite as if he were a
bad risk, or a Captain Sharp who fuzzed the cards.
He, the Marquess of Rockford!

The lights were still on downstairs when he arrived. Still, he used his key, slamming the door
shut behind him. Lucy appeared at the parlor door.
She looked apprehensive.

"Lor', you did give me a start, M'lord," she
scolded him before she remembered to smile.

"Why should that be?" he demanded as he
walked by her and threw himself down in a chair.
"This is my house, and I am the only gentleman to
come here, am I not?"

Realizing that the marquess was in a blazing
temper, Lucy made herself laugh lightly. "Of course
you are," she said as she went to pour him a glass
of wine. It was all she could think of to do, for she
was feeling most uneasy. She had seen Nick Sinclair out of temper before, of course, but she had
never seen such a glaring light in his narrowed
eyes, nor had his mouth ever been set in such a
grim line. She did not like the way he was
clenching his fists, either, and she resolved to keep
her distance until he calmed down.

Accordingly she took a seat across from him after she had brought him his wine. He stared down at it as if he had never seen anything like it before, and didn't quite know what to do with it. Which was, she told herself, ridiculous. He had had his vintner deliver the wine here himself, since he considered her incapable of choosing anything worthy of his palate.

At last he tossed it down and grimaced. Lucy searched her mind for something to say to divert him, but nothing occurred to her. And she really did not think this was the best time to remind him he had not given her this month's housekeeping money, or reimbursed her for her labors.

"I am surprised to see you here at this hour," she said finally as the silence between them lengthened. Silence from one of her gentlemen made Lucy nervous. "It is so early, is it not? Not that I'm not always delighted to see you, whenever you come, sir," she added quickly as he glared at her. "Er, what would you care to do? Perhaps a game of cards?"

"You must be the only person in town who dares play with me," he muttered, running a hand through his dark hair. "No, thank you, however. You've no skill, and therefore aren't a challenge."

"But I've other kinds of skills, isn't that so, Nicky?" she dared to say pertly as she glanced sideways at him under her lashes.

"Don't call me Nicky! I've told you that before! As for skill, why, yes, to be sure you do."

He fell silent then, for it had suddenly occurred to him that the skill Lucy referred to was her only talent. But then, to be fair to her, he had hardly installed her here because she was a brilliant conversationalist.

As she came to stand before him, he pulled her down on his lap and kissed her long and hard, hoping she could help him forget the insulting rejection he had just received. A rejection he knew would be all over town tomorrow. For even if Duke Ainsworth held his tongue, that doorkeeper would be sure to tell others about it when they arrived at or left the house.

But tonight all Lucy's considerable skill could not make him forget for long the slight he had received. And long after she fell asleep in the big four-poster upstairs, he lay beside her, staring up into the dark at the canopy he could not see, brooding about it.

What had happened to make him so sure of success all at once? he wondered. It was weird, unexplainable. All those things people were saying were true. He rarely lost, no, not even when he deliberately set out to do so. But he had made no pact with the devil. To be truthful, he did not believe in the devil, or in God, or in heaven or hell. They were abstracts, and therefore difficult to fathom for a man who required proof before he could say a-men and a-men. Yet there had to be *something* causing his endless good fortune that had driven other gamblers away from him.

He grimaced then, annoyed with himself. He sounded like a little boy, whining because others would not play with him! Be a man, he told himself sternly. This state of affairs cannot last much longer. It's just a matter of waiting it out.

Lucy cuddled closer, throwing one rounded arm across his chest. Gently he removed that arm. He wanted no contact with her now. To his relief she did not wake, but only sighed a little before she turned over on her side away from him.

For some reason Victoria Emerson's face came to

mind, and he wondered why. True, she had looked especially beautiful tonight in her sea-green silk. The gown had been cut low across the bosom, exposing a great deal of her soft skin. He recalled the gentle rose of her flushed complexion, the little black curls that clustered on her brow, and he wondered what it would have been like if he had had her in his arms tonight, instead of the practiced Lucy.

He shook his head. There was no chance of that! Why had such an incongruous thought come to mind? Of course, he admitted that Miss Emerson intrigued him as no other young lady ever had. He fully intended that their next encounter would not consist only of sly remarks. He knew she had a lively mind. A real conversation with her would be far from boring, and far from the usual sparring between the sexes that passed for conversation in the ton. The same kind they had had tonight. But never again, he promised himself.

Miss Emerson had impressed him with her poise. Why, look how she had given as good as she got tonight, how quickly she had answered all his verbal challenges. And to think she had even ordered him to open the door! But why, he asked himself, had he been so quick to obey?

He yawned and stretched, deciding to go home. He had no desire to see Lucy in the clear light of dawn, and dawn was not far off. As he slid from bed, she made a little sound. He ignored her as he pulled on his clothes without lighting a candle. Before he quit the room, he left a large sum of money on the dresser. Remembering how Lucy had reminded him of his debt to her right after their lovemaking made him grimace now. In spite of all her fervent declarations of love, Lucy didn't have an ounce of romance in her soul. She was as practical as anybody else when it came to getting good value for her services.

As he walked home, he wrinkled his nose in disgust. Even at this hour, London stank of coal smoke, garbage, and its reeking open sewers. Strange that he should notice it now, he thought. Surely he was used to it. It must be because the pearl-gray morning was so perfect with promise that the odor seemed twice as offensive.

It was at that moment Nick Sinclair decided to go down to the country. He had no engagements he could not break, and he felt he would be better for the reprieve. Besides, if he were not in town, he would not have to hear the whispers, nor reply to all the knowing remarks and sly smiles about how he had become anathema at the tables.

Yes, he would sleep for a few hours and then be off to the southern coast and Tye. It was his smallest seat, but he had always thought it his loveliest. And the sea air would blow away all these depressing thoughts he had been having.

As for Miss Victoria Emerson, well, what was she to him, after all? And she was sure to be here still when he returned.

Five hours later, Marquess Rockford set out in his racing curricle behind his highbred pair. His new tiger was perched beside him on the narrow seat. His valet would follow later at a slower pace with his clothes and such delicacies from town as might make his stay at Tye more pleasant.

"This place we're going to, is it far?" Toby asked after a long spell of silence.

"It's near Weymouth. We should make it in two days' time if the weather holds," the marquess told him, staring straight ahead as he guided the team by a lumbering farm cart.

"But why are you leaving London?" the boy asked next.

Nick Sinclair stared down at him for a second, astonished at his boldness. "It is not your place to inquire why I do anything," he said coldly. "My business is none of your affair. You go where I go, with no questions asked, and I'll thank you to remember it."

"Just thought to pass the time of day. No offense meant, guv," Toby was quick to reply. "Er, look out for that old carriage, now."

"I see it. Do you think I need your instruction?"

" 'Course not. What I do think is that you're in a bad temper, so I shall hold my tongue."

"Wise of you!" came the terse reply.

True to his word, Toby did not say another word until they stopped to rest the team and partake of a rough meal of bread and cheese at a roadside inn.

Later that afternoon, Toby suddenly asked the marquess to pull over.

"Got to go awful bad, sir," he said, looking beseeching.

The marquess pulled the team to a halt at the side of the road. He waved an impatient hand, not at all pleased, for he had just been passed by an elegant chaise driven by a fellow wearing a coat with at least ten capes on it. His impudent grin had clearly challenged the marquess to a race.

Now, of course, due to Toby's unfortunate timing, there was little chance he could catch the man up. Still, he told himself as he slumped a little on the uncomfortable seat, it was just as well. There was no chance he could have lost. Nor would I even without this cursed good luck I'm saddled with, he told himself. He would bet his pair against any, most certainly that flashy team that was being driven by such a down-the-road fellow.

Idly he stared at the woods where Toby had disappeared. But where could the lad be? Surely his call of nature was taking a very long time. He was about to call out when the tiger came into sight, a wide grin on his face.

"I do pray you are completely comfortable, sir?" the marquess inquired as Toby climbed to his seat and they set off again.

Toby only grinned even more widely, and the marquess fell silent. He was deep in himself now, not even noticing the lovely spring countryside, a hundred tender shades of new green. Nor did he hear the birdsong that filled every hedge. A few wildflowers were in bloom, and their scent was certainly more pleasant than London's, yet he did not remark on it.

A few miles farther on, he came upon some people standing in the road, while more were running toward them from a nearby field, and he pulled his team to a halt. To his horror, he saw that the man who had challenged him to race had come to grief on a narrow bridge that spanned a rushing stream.

One of the yokels was pulling the man from the water. His head was bloody, and he was ominously still. One of the horses lay almost submerged in the water, as still as his master, while the other struggled to escape the harness.

The marquess opened his mouth to order his tiger to go and help, but there was no need, for Toby was already halfway down the bank.

The yokel laid the dead man on the bank, shaking his head as he straightened. Behind Nick

Sinclair several field hands were whispering together.

"You there! What happened here?" he demanded of the man who had tried to rescue the driver.

"I'm not sure, sir," the yokel said, coming closer and removing his hat. "I wuz workin' in the field there when I heard a crash-like. The carriage went over, them horses neighing in fright. By the time I got 'ere, the gent were dead. Drowned-like. As ter *why* there wuz an accident, I can't rightly say. True, we've had a deal o' rain this spring. Mebbe the bridge supports let go. Or mebbe the man come ter grief by the railin' lettin' go. 'Ard ter say."

"You had best take his body to the nearest justice and tell him what happened," Sinclair ordered. He could see Toby had the remaining horse free now, and was leading it up the banking. As he did so, he talked to it quietly. The horse was docile enough now. Toby's miraculous touch, the marquess thought.

It was some little time before Sinclair could be on his way again. He had to be sure the man's papers were safe, so he could be identified. And he wanted to see the body disposed in the cart before he left. As well, he took charge of getting what remained of the chaise pulled from the stream, and the dead horse as well. It was a thoroughly depressing matter.

It was necessary to take a detour of several miles before another bridge was reached. For a while the marquess brooded over the accident. At last he shrugged. The man must have been a ham-handed driver to come to grief even on a narrow bridge. Just as well he had not agreed to a race.

It was late the following day before the pair arrived at the gates of Tye. As they passed between them and bowled up the long drive, Toby looked about with interest. "Nice place you got here, guv," he said.

"I cannot tell you how relieved I am that it meets with your approval," his master said coldly.

"Seems to me a man could be happy here all year-round," the tiger persisted. "Look at that big house, those fields sloping to the beach! And all those fruit trees! A sight it is!"

The marquess did not reply, and he added with a sideways glance, " 'Course it would be even nicer if you had a wife, don't you think? Why don't you get married, guv?"

There was a long, pregnant pause before the marquess said, "Be very careful. You can so easily be replaced."

What Toby might have said in reply was not known, for just then they pulled up before a rambling brick house and he was forced to run to the horses' heads. As the marquess climbed down and stretched his cramped body, he wondered anew why he put up with such sass. Surely even the lad's magical touch with horses couldn't excuse his boldness.

But he forgot Toby the minute he entered the wide hall of the mansion, a hall that stretched from the front door clear to the back where it opened on a handsome stone terrace. Several large pots of blooming spring flowers had been placed there. Tye's butler was bowing and smiling a greeting, having been alerted to his master's arrival by a groom who had come on ahead. All was ready to welcome the Baron of Tye home.

As he sat in a drawing room enjoying a glass of wine before he went to change his clothes, Nick Sinclair recalled Toby's cheeky remark about a wife, and he snorted. Why on earth would he saddle himself with such a distasteful responsibility when he was so indulged by his excellent staff? he asked himself. The mansion was spotless, its furniture gleaming with beeswax and care. To his nostrils came the distant aroma of fresh-baked bread and a roast sizzling on the spit, and he was reminded how hungry he was. The window beside him was open, and he could hear some songbirds in the garden. Down on the beach, seagulls cried as they searched the shallows for their dinner. Sinclair promised himself he would visit the beach tomorrow, as he took the spyglass down from the mantel to search the distant horizon. It was something he had done since boyhood, watching the ships that sailed by, and wondering where they had been and where they were going. No wonder he loved Tye so much. It was a beautiful place. And, he reminded himself, one that did not need further adornment by the addition of a member of the opposite sex.

He was happy in the days that followed. Out early every fine day, he rode his acres, oversaw the spring planting, and conferred with his agent. Since everything was running smoothly under that man's direction, Sinclair had a great deal of free time on his hands, and he amused himself by fishing, drawing up plans for a possible glasshouse, and walking the beach. Once he came upon Toby there, just staring out to sea. When he asked what he was thinking of, he received what he considered an evasive answer. He could have pressed the lad, insisted on the truth, but for some reason he hesitated to do so. Perhaps because he never knew what Toby would say, and he really did not want to let him go, no matter how many times he had threatened to do so.

Now, a little tired of his own company, he suggested Toby walk the beach with him; obediently the tiger joined him. Every once in a while he would pick up a shell and examine it before he dropped it to the sand again. Once Nick Sinclair was sure he heard him sigh.

"Is there something on your mind, Toby?" he found himself asking.

The contemplative look on the lad's round, freckled face was gone in a flash. "No, guv, nothing at all," he said in haste. "I was just remembering something. Look there, sir! Isn't that what they call a packet out there?"

Successfully diverted, the marquess stared out to sea. "You must have excellent eyesight to see that. Without my telescope, I can barely make out a sail," he said.

"I was just thinking how nice it would be for the horses if they were brought down here on hot summer days for a swim. 'Course you'd have to wash the salt off after, but I think they'd like it, don't you, guv?"

"Those that wouldn't be spooked by the waves. I had a mare once who panicked every time I tried to ride her along the beach."

"Oh, you mean *Lia*, don't you, guv? The black mare with the white blaze?"

The marquess paused, a flat stone in his hand. "How did you know about *Lia*? That mare died of the strangles two years ago. Long before your time."

" 'Course she did," Toby said. "Or so one of the grooms here told me."

The marquess nodded and sent his stone spinning. It skipped five times before it sank, and he grinned a little, pleased he hadn't lost his touch.

When the two returned to the house late that afternoon, Nick Sinclair was newly tanned and tired. As for Toby, he had acquired another hundred freckles or so, and his red curls blazed with added fire.

"Surely the devil had a hand in the color of your hair, lad," the marquess teased at the bottom of the steps.

"The devil didn't have a thing to do with it, guv," Toby retorted with his cheeky grin. Before Sinclair could call him to task, he was away, running toward the stables.

Seven

ONLY FOUR DAYS later, Nick Sinclair was on his way back to London. He had grown restless, not so much with the sleepy pace of country life, as with his own company. He associated with few of his neighbors, and of course, he only spoke to his servants to give them an order. As for Toby, even though he found his tiger engaging, even amusing, he had come to see that encouraging him just led to more of his impudence.

Besides, it was mid-May now. He had been gone for two weeks. Surely any talk about him being turned away from Mrs. Tandy's must have died down. And there was Clarissa Carr's garden fete to attend. He was looking forward to seeing Victoria Emerson there.

He wondered if she had missed him. But perhaps she had not even noticed he was gone. What a depressing thought, he told himself with a rueful grin. He was surprised to discover how much he hoped she had noticed, and missed him as well. But of course, he reassured himself, he only felt that way because of the score he still had to settle with her father. Strangely he did not waste a thought on his mistress, neither to wonder how she was faring, nor how it would be when he had her in his arms again.

As he stopped his dusty curricle before his house on Park Lane, and Toby ran to take the horses in charge, he saw a smiling Bart Whitaker approaching.

"Well met, sir," that gentleman said as he extended his hand. "I heard you'd left town. Nothing serious, I trust?"

"Not a bit of it, but come in and join me in a glass. I've the dust of several roads in my throat. Toby, take 'em around and be sure to give them a good rubdown."

His tiger's stare was severe. " 'Course I will," he said indignantly. "Not stupid, y'know."

"Does he always speak to you like that?" Whitaker asked in some amazement as the two climbed the shallow steps, and a smoldering Toby led the team away to the mews.

Nick Sinclair sighed. "For my sins he does. Truly, I would not put up with it except he's such a hand with horseflesh. Ah, Geary, some burgundy in the library, at once.

"I shall expect you to tell me all the town news, Whitaker," he added as he led the way to that room and his butler hurried off on his errand. "I feel I've been gone an age. And you, as I know full well, are sure to have all the latest gossip at your fingertips."

"Well, now, let me see," his guest said easily as he took the seat the marquess indicated. "The Duke of Hefton and his wife had a battle royal the other evening at the theater. I am told it was much more amusing than the performance on stage. It seems the duchess took exception to the amount of attention her beloved bestowed on one of the opera dancers, and the kiss the young lady blew in his direction. And although the duke has always claimed she was a distant cousin newly arrived from the colonies when he married her, it is said the duchess sounded exactly like the serving wench so many claimed she once was.

"It is also common knowledge that Tony Kingsley is about to bring his wife up on a crim-con case. He'll name Mark Dedhamson, of course. And two nights ago, Angus McCree broke the bank at Mrs. Tandy's."

Sinclair smiled. "How satisfying that news is," he said.

"Yes, I heard about you being turned away at the door. Still having the devil's own luck?"

"How would I know? No one will play with me."

"You really can't expect them to, sir," Whitaker pointed out. "One wagers on the chance of a win, but never when one knows a win is impossible."

Nick Sinclair threw out his hands. "But, of course, it would be unreasonable of me to expect any different treatment, now, wouldn't it?"

"Have you any idea why you have suddenly become so lucky?" Whitaker persisted, after the butler had served them and departed. "I must tell you there are those in London who insist there's something more afoot than plain good luck, and there's a lot of them wondering what the secret is to your success. I'd watch my back, if I were you, Sinclair. Someone might be desperate enough to kidnap you and force you to reveal that secret."

His host laughed, long and hard. "But there's no secret, none at all," he said when he could speak again. "I've no idea why I suddenly can't lose. I've even tried to, believe it or not. Please tell people I employ no wiles, and there's been no dark dealings. And I am sure, before very long, this miraculous streak of good luck of mine will change. It's bound to. It always has before."

He changed the subject then, but he was not sorry when Whitaker took his leave a short time later. He had seen a knowing look on his guest's face when he denied all knowledge of his good fortune, and he had resented it. It was almost as if Whitaker believed he was being put off; that he, Rockford, truly had found some secret way to win which he was refusing to reveal.

He went to his desk to inspect the cards of invitation that had arrived in his absence. He saw there were a number of parties he was bidden to attend in the next few days, and he wondered if Victoria Emerson would be at any of them.

But Miss Emerson was not among the crowds at the soiree that evening, nor was she at a reception he looked in on later. Nick Sinclair told himself it was ridiculous to feel such disappointment. London society was not so large that he could not be sure to meet her sooner or later. Unless, of course, the family had returned to the country. But surely if they had, Whitaker would have mentioned it.

Sinclair toyed with the idea of visiting Lucy, but at last he decided against it and went home early, to the delight and approval of his long-suffering servants.

Perhaps it was his unusually early bedtime that found him awake before eight the following morning. It promised to be a fair day, and only half an hour later he rode his horse to Hyde Park for an early canter. He had completed a circuit of Rotten Row when he noticed a horsewoman approaching from the opposite direction. To his satisfaction, it was Victoria Emerson, quite alone except for an attendant groom. He raised his hand and halted, forcing her to do the same.

"But what a delight to see you about at this hour, Miss Emerson," he said, bowing a little and giving her a warm smile. She looked different to him this morning, and he wondered at it. More natural somehow, more approachable.

Tory patted her roan's neck and smiled in return, but inwardly she was seething. Why, oh, why had she put on this old country habit? she wondered. And why had she merely pulled her hair back and tied it carelessly with a ribbon? The marquess, of course, looked complete to a shade. No doubt, he would do so at any hour of the day or night, damn him!

"I always try to ride early, sir," she made herself say. "It is so much more enjoyable without others to consider. And my mare has yet to become accustomed to town. She also prefers solitude."

Ignoring this blatant hint that he take himself off, Sinclair nodded as he wheeled his horse. "I couldn't agree more," he said easily. "Shall we canter?"

Tory could do nothing but nod distantly. She could hardly refuse his escort, not without giving the groom something to talk about. And from the other servants to Essie and her mother and father was but a very small step.

She was glad she rode well enough to feel easy in such a wonderful horseman's presence. The marquess seemed almost part of his mount. At his signal, she slowed her mare to a trot. The groom had dropped behind a little, which ensured their privacy.

"I have been out of town. Dare I hope you noticed my absence and missed me?" Sinclair asked with a smile, determined not to miss this unforeseen opportunity to advance his suit.

Tory bit back a startled gasp at his boldness, and tried to ignore the warmth of that smile.

"I am afraid I did not, sir," she said, staring straight ahead again. "But then, I would not be apt to, would I? We are mere acquaintances, and I have met so many people here. I declare London grows more populated every day."

"Yes, it does. And there are any number of other innocuous boring bits of frivolous conversation we could engage in. But I think not, Miss Emerson. I found I missed you. It is one of the reasons I hurried back here. Are you flattered? You should be, you know. I rarely bother with young ladies in their first season."

"I assure you, I am having the greatest trouble containing my joy, sir," she answered promptly. "Such condescension is unnerving. I pray I do not swoon."

He chuckled. "That's repaid me in spades, hasn't it? You don't sound a bit unnerved, and I'll wager you've never fainted in your life. You've a great deal of composure for one your age, and almost too much poise. I wonder what it would take to truly unbalance you? I'm tempted to try."

"Instead try not to be so ridiculous, m'lord," she snapped. "I beg you to leave me now. I've no desire for any more of this—this conversation."

"Or of me?" he asked, making no move to obey her. "How unkind of you when I have just admitted I am smitten. From what Whitaker tells me, you are no stranger to men in that condition. Surely you would not send me away so cruelly?"

Tory continued to stare between the mare's ears. She would not look at him, she told herself. He was entirely too free for her liking, and this admiration he claimed must surely be false. He barely knew her, nor she, him. Still, she could not help being conscious of his tall, lean body sitting his horse so easily, those strong hands in their tight gloves firm on the reins. Even without looking she could picture his rugged face in her mind's eye, those broad shoulders under his riding jacket, the strong chin and well-cut mouth—those mesmerizing gray eyes. To her disgust she could not help darting a quick glance at him, as if to make sure she was remembering him correctly.

"Yes, I am considered a well-enough looking man, I believe," she heard him say, and she wondered if he could read minds. "Not, of course, as handsome as some, and nowhere near equal to your beauty, but passable.

"I did not see you last night, and I looked for you at both the Booth-Locke's soiree, and Lady Waring's reception. They were pleasant parties, but since you did not grace them, in no way unusual."

"We attended a concert last evening," Tory said. Then, to change the subject, she added, "I have heard you are a great gamester, sir. One who suddenly cannot lose. How comes this about?"

"Not you, too," he said, a little exasperated. "I've not the slightest clue, my dear. And I dislike the notoriety it has brought me if it has even come to your adorable ears. But as I told your good friend Bart Whitaker yesterday, I am sure it will disappear as quickly as it came. And I shall not be at all sorry to see it go. It has been downright peculiar—unnerving."

"Why do you gamble?" she asked, slowing her mare to a walk and staring openly at him now. She did not pursue the subject merely to keep him from flirting with her. She really did want to know.

He shrugged, a frown on his face. "It is something to do to pass the time. And I enjoy it. It is exciting wondering what the next card dealt will be, or how the die will fall."

Remembering how her father had said the marquess was gambling his fortune away, made Tory say, "But it is such a useless occupation, gambling. And it can lead to such great evil."

"Never tell me you are a puritan, ma'am. Or worse still, a reformer. No, no, I do not believe it. Not someone as lovely as you!"

"I could have no reason to want to reform you," she said quietly. "I was only wondering, for I know it is an occupation a great many gentlemen indulge in, sometimes to their ruin. And I cannot for the life of me understand why they do so."

"You do not understand because you're not a gambler, ma'am," he told her. "Just as well for you. It is an expensive pastime."

"My father says ... well, I do not suppose you are interested in his views on the subject, so I shall not bore you with them."

She looked around and saw they had reached the Stanhope Gate, and in some relief, she signaled her groom before she added, "I must leave you now. I have a number of errands to do today, and I am already late."

"I shall look for you some other fine morning, Miss Emerson," the marquess said easily. "Riding with you is a delightful way to begin the day. Give you good morning, ma'am."

He watched her ride away, her back very straight, as if she knew she was under observation.

She had a supple waist, and an elegant spine. Altogether, she was a thoroughly delectable piece.

For some reason he remembered Lucy then, and he frowned a little. He supposed he should go and see how she was doing even though he had no desire at the moment to make love to her. Strange, that. He had never been fond of celibacy, and here it had been almost three weeks since he had been with her.

When he reached the little house where he had installed her, he beckoned to an urchin to watch his horse, before he sounded the knocker. Lucy's maid's eyes widened when she saw him, and she was quick to bob a curtsy and scurry off toward the kitchen.

The marquess looked in the parlor before he took the stairs two at a time. "Lucy? Where are you hiding, wench?" he called as he threw the bedroom door open.

His smile faded as he heard her gasp, and saw how she crouched on the carpet before her trunk, a muslin gown held tightly in her trembling hands.

"Well, now, and what's all this?" he asked softly as he closed the door and leaned against it, his arms crossed over his chest. The room was in a state of great disarray. Gowns and shifts, shawls and pelisses, were spread over every surface. All her bonnets were stacked on a chair, and a pile of sandals leaned drunkenly against a large portmanteau. Even the dressing table had been swept clean of bottles of scent, her comb and brush and hand mirror. "Going somewhere, Lucy?" he asked, still in that deceptively mild voice.

She swallowed and rose to her feet, never taking her eyes from his face. "Yes, I am. You haven't been here for ever so long, and I, well, I got tired o' wait-ing fer you. *For* you."

"Did you indeed," he remarked, straightening up and coming toward her. She darted behind a large wing chair, and he chuckled.

"Oh, come, girl! I'm not about to hurt you! If you want to go, that's your privilege."

Deciding he meant her no harm, she tossed her head and came back to her trunk. "You've got a temper on you, m'lord. I wasn't sure how you'd take my leaving. Better safe than sorry, you know."

"Where will you go, Lucy?" he asked idly. "I wouldn't want you to suffer in any way."

She looked away from him till all he could see was the curve of her cheek, half hidden in a tangle of curls. "Thank you," she whispered. "I'll—I'll be all right."

"Never tell me you've found another protector so soon? My congratulations, ma'am. Such foresight must be applauded."

Lucy bristled at his mocking tone, and she said hotly, "Yes, you can laugh all you like, m'fine lord. But I have to take care of m'self, I do. You've been growing tired of me for quite a while now. I could tell. And when that happens, a girl who knows what's what, looks about her quick, she does."

"Well, this is a new come-out for me," the mar-quess mused as he handed her another gown. "I'm generally the one who does the dismissing. I shall try to survive the snub, however."

Lucy folded the gown and laid it in the trunk. "Oh, you'll survive it, all right," she said, nodding sagely. "I just hope you meet your match one day, Nicky. Not that I expect that to happen. Not in this world anyway. You're a deal too quick and much too full of yourself to love only one woman. Still, I'd give a lot, if you found yourself 'cotched,' I would."

She stood up then and closed the trunk. "I'll be off later today," she said briskly. "You'll find all in order after I'm gone."

His smile lit his gray eyes, and she added, "I'm still here now, though. That is, if you'd care to, Nicky . . . for old times' sake, like?"

The marquess decided there was no point scolding her for the use of his nickname, not when she'd be gone so shortly. And he wondered at the feeling of relief he had, knowing that to be so.

"No, but thank you, Lucy. I find I'm not in the mood for dalliance today. Take care of yourself. And if you'll heed a word of advice, save your money. You're going to need it one of these days."

He dropped his heavy purse on the dressing table and left the room. Lucy stood very still until she heard the front door close behind him. Only then did she hurry to the window to watch him mount his horse and ride away down the street.

It was too bad. He had been special. But although her new protector was much older and nowhere near as physically attractive as Rockford, he had great wealth and had recently been widowed. And you never knew with men like that. Turned silly, some of them did. She intended to do her best to see he fell in love with her. Then, perhaps, she might even be "m'lady" someday, surrounded by servants to do her bidding, smothered in jewels and wearing rich clothes. Save her money, indeed!

Why, she might even have the pleasure of watching the Marquess of Rockford make his bow to her. After all, stranger things had happened, now hadn't they?

Eight

THE MORNING OF Lady Clarissa Carr's garden fete dawned bright and sunny, to Victoria Emerson's relief and delight. If it had looked the least bit threatening, she was sure her father would have insisted she remain at home, using as an excuse his fear she might catch a chill. But now he would not have that excuse. She ate her breakfast in bed while her maid took out the gown she had chosen to wear. It was white as her hostess had requested, but Tory hoped it was distinctive enough to stand out in a crowd. The round neckline was trimmed with beautiful, fragile white lace, and matching lace banded the tiny puffed sleeves, and the hem as well. Tory had a new hat to wear, a broad-brimmed white straw crowned with white roses and tied with white satin ribbons. Even her sandals and hose, her kid gloves and parasol, were pristine white.

She was ready long before Lady Garen's carriage arrived, so she was forced to count to ten a number of times while her mother and father both instructed her as to how she should go on. Be patient, she reminded herself. Remember they do this because they love you.

At last the butler announced the carriage, and Tory rose to kiss them before she said, "Now, don't fret! You know I am perfectly safe in Anne's company, Papa, truly. As for watching my manners, Mama, well, do you think to insult yourself? After all, you have been teaching them to me since I was a small girl. Shame on you!"

She laughed at them both and ran away over her mother's protests that she had never meant such a thing, and Victoria knew it.

"Now, why does it appear to me that you have just escaped something dire by the skin of your teeth?" Anne Garen asked as Tory climbed into the carriage and settled down beside her.

"Is it so obvious? But I *have* escaped. Mama and Papa both have been nattering at me for the past half hour. I was almost sure they would discover some reason I could not go, so I flew out the door!"

Her cousin smiled. "Yes, they are overprotective, I know. But you must remember it is a great thing, love. You are fortunate. Some people are never loved that way by anyone all their lives. Be grateful, and forgive their fussing."

A little surprised at how serious Anne was, Tory nodded. "I know you are right, cuz, and I do try. But come, let us forget them and enjoy ourselves. Isn't it grand that it turned out a fair day?"

The drive to Richmond was beguiled by a conversation that ranged over a number of subjects, from plays and books, to parties and the ton itself.

"Are you still enthralled with it?" Anne asked as the carriage neared their destination. "You do remember that I said you would tire of its platitudes, its gossip, its conceit. Aren't you bored yet?"

"Not yet, I'm afraid, but don't despise me! I admit I have on occasion found my mind wandering when some sprig of fashion deigns to converse with me. And sometimes I find I am standing a bit apart, as if I were merely an observer. I have heard some truly silly things said. And in perfect seriousness, too."

Her cousin chuckled. "I'm glad you have kept your sense of humor, my dear. Ah, I see we have arrived," she added as the carriage turned in between a pair of massive stone pillars and bowled up a winding drive. On either side of that drive, rhododendrons were in full bloom, all pink and white and purple.

Victoria Emerson looked around in awe as she stepped from the carriage moments later. She could see that the gardens were extensive, and filled with spring flowers. Some couples were strolling there, the ladies in their white gowns a perfect foil for the flowers' brilliant color.

Beyond the gardens, green velvet lawns stretched down to the banks of the Thames where there was a dainty gazebo, a boathouse and a small landing. There were people on the river already, and Miss Emerson's smile was pure delight.

Lady Carr waited at the top of the steps to greet her guests. Anne Garen wondered at the intent look she gave Tory; how she held her hands for some time while she studied her and listened to her thanks for the invitation. At last the older lady let her go and turned to her companion.

"Now I know the day is a success since you attend, Lady Garen," she teased, one hand smoothing her soft white hair as a little breeze came up.

Anne smiled in reply. "Dear ma'am, I would not have missed this gala for the world. And only you could have produced such a glorious day for it."

"We will be having an alfresco nuncheon in an hour or so," Lady Carr said, smiling from one to the other. "Until then, do feel free to amuse yourself as you wish. I don't imagine this young lady will lack for an escort long, do you, m'lady? Indeed, I see one hurrying toward her even now."

Tory told herself she would not look around, or appear eager in any way. Of course the Marquess of Rockford had probably been invited. She had fully expected to see him here, had even been looking forward to it. But he must never know that.

To her chagrin, Lord Dorr bowed before her, his good-natured face wearing a beaming smile of satisfaction. Tory told herself the disappointment she felt was absurd.

"Run along, my dear," Anne murmured. "I see some old friends in the garden, and I shall join them for a while."

Tory took Lord Dorr's arm, and when he asked, told him she would very much like to walk down to the river. As they strolled along, she heard the sounds of a string quartet playing in the gazebo, and she smiled. There was also a tent with attendant maids for the ladies if they wished to retire, and footmen carrying laden trays offered the guests wine and fruit punch. Truly Lady Carr had thought of everything for her guests' amusement and comfort. It was an enviable talent she had.

"You are looking very beautiful today. In fact, you take my breath away, Miss Emerson," Lord Dorr said, bending over her to whisper.

"Now, m'lord, you know I have told you I do not care to hear such extravagant compliments," she scolded, but she smiled as she spoke, which took the sting from her words.

"I can't help it," he said simply, his hand coming up to capture hers where it lay on his arm.

"If you do not behave yourself, I shall leave you," Tory warned. She had been fending off the young viscount's advances almost from first meeting, so he did not alarm her. She could wish, however, he was not so tireless in his pursuit.

"Come now, can't we just enjoy this wonderful party?" she coaxed. "Promise me you will restrain yourself, at least for today."

Lord Dorr sighed, but he did remove his hand. "Very well. I would do anything for you, Miss Emerson, and you know it. So, although it will be very hard, I'll obey you. But I warn you, the next time we meet, I intend to be more direct with you."

Tory did not care about "next time" today. It was too far in the future to worry about.

When they reached the banks of the river, they joined a group near the gazebo who were listening to the music. Some of the older ladies had lawn chairs, while the younger ones relaxed on large cushions provided by the servants. Tory arranged her parasol to shield her face from the sun, and prepared to enjoy the concert.

But not many minutes later, she felt distinctly uneasy, sure someone was staring at her. When she looked around, she saw the Marquess of Rockford coming toward her, his eyes intent on her face.

"Miss Emerson," he said, bowing a little before he sat down on the lawn beside her. On her other side, Lord Dorr glared at him, but the marquess ignored him. "I have looked for you in the park and at various parties, but somehow or other we never seem to meet. No matter. We are both here today. You will honor me at nuncheon, won't you?"

He was not asking a question, as Tory knew very well. Next to her, Lord Dorr sputtered his indignation. Unfortunately he was incoherent.

"No, I will not," Tory said. "I am joining my cousin Anne."

"But of course Lady Garen will be one of our

party," Nick Sinclair assured her in his smoothest voice. Tory longed to hit him. "I have already arranged it with her and some of her friends. I am sure you will find them fascinating. They are older, therefore worldlier." He paused to glance at the red-faced young viscount before he added, "And infinitely more articulate.

"M'lord? If you will excuse us?"

He rose and held out his hand to Tory. She wanted desperately to refuse his escort, but she could see several of the guests were staring now, waiting to see what she would do. Taking his hand, she found herself lifted to her feet with no effort at all, and a moment later found that same hand tucked in his arm as he led her up the lawn to the gardens.

"You are angry with me," Sinclair remarked, bowing slightly to Lady Wills who was eyeing his companion coldly. Tory did not even notice.

"Oh, how can you think that?" she asked sweetly. "Why, I just adore being manipulated by arrogant gentlemen who are so intent on satisfying their own wishes, they never consider mine."

He led her under a grape arbor before he answered. Even this early in the spring, the new green leaves formed an effective curtain, hiding them from view. There was no one else in the arbor. They were quite alone.

"Yes, I suppose I am arrogant," he admitted a little ruefully. "And used to getting my own way. But tell me, Miss Emerson, when you were a little girl, did you ever play pretend?"

Perplexed at the change of subject, she nodded. "Of course. What child has not?"

"I did, too. I could be a pirate, a soldier, even a bird in my imagination. Of course, what I really wanted to be was a highwayman, and, barring that, a groom," he confided. Tory smiled a little.

"I suggest we try and recapture our childhood days. Each of us pretend, just for this one, magical day, that we are in perfect accord. You forget my reputation as a rake and a gambler—my arrogance. I'll forget your mistrust of me, your reserve. Can you do that?"

He leaned closer, and Tory was startled. He was much too near. Why, she could feel his warm breath on her cheek. Then she scoffed at herself. What could Rockford possibly do to her in broad daylight at a crowded garden party?

It took only a moment to find out. Taking her chin in his hand, he tipped it up even though she continued to stare at him. She saw him glance at her mouth before he moved closer still. As his lips touched hers, she closed her eyes.

Tory Emerson had been kissed once or twice before. They had been furtive, inept kisses delivered by infatuated young men from whom she had struggled to escape. Rockford's kiss was nothing at all like them. For one thing it was warm and tender and accomplished. And although it did not threaten her, it was insistent. Far from wanting to escape it, Tory was having the greatest difficulty keeping her hands by her sides, when she really wanted to put her arms around his neck—melt against him. When he raised his head at last and she slowly opened her eyes, she saw a light deep in his gray ones. She put her fingertips to her lips in awe.

What was happening to her? she wondered. Nicholas Sinclair—the Marquess of Rockford—was not a good man. She should not listen to him, or be with him, and most certainly she should never have permitted that kiss.

But wouldn't it be wonderful to do as he suggested? Just for today? Wouldn't it be wonderful to get to know him—his past, his hopes, his dreams?

"It is not such a difficult thing I ask, is it?" he murmured, interrupting her reverie. "Not an impossible one? Say yes, Victoria. Say yes."

"Yes," she said, before she could have second thoughts. "Yes, I will pretend with you, m'lord."

To her surprise, he grinned broadly. "Good girl! Best we vacate this convenient spot, don't you agree? Someone else might want to enjoy its privacy."

As they left the arbor, he said, "Shall we go out on the river after the picnic? Or would you prefer to inspect the gardens?"

"The river by all means. Gardens can be seen anytime," she said, wondering why she felt so happy, so carefree. "You do row, don't you? I will be safe?"

He pretended to be indignant. "You dare ask? I am an expert!"

She laughed up at him, her eyes dancing as she shook her head as if to scold him for his conceit.

Up on the broad terrace overlooking the festivities, Lady Carr and her friend, the Duchess of Norwood, watched the pair with a great deal of interest.

"I say, Clarissa, wouldn't it be grand if Nicky and that pretty gel were to make a match of it?" the duchess demanded, unabashedly raising her lorgnette for a closer inspection.

"Indeed, it would," her hostess agreed. "And it just might be the making of him, too."

"Good family? A respectable dowry? She's in good health?" the duchess persisted.

"An excellent family. They are related to the Earl of Landover, and the Oxfordshire Faynes. Miss Emerson is an only child. She will inherit all. And from what I could see this morning, she is in blooming good health."

"Why, it couldn't be better," the duchess said, lowering her lorgnette at last. "But he's probably only flirting with her. You know how averse Nicky is to matrimony."

"I don't know about that," Clarissa Carr said slowly. "He was the one who asked me to give this fete, and he especially requested Miss Emerson receive an invitation."

"My word!" the duchess exclaimed, properly impressed. "However, knowing Nicky Sinclair as well as I do, I don't think I shall get my wedding finery ready quite yet.

"I say, Clarissa, why is the Countess of Wills looking so black? Have you heard anything there that I might have missed?"

Nine

I<small>T WAS A</small> truly wonderful day, one that Tory knew she would remember even when she was a very old lady. She and the marquess had joined Anne and her friends for nuncheon on some benches under a massive oak. The conversation had been quick—witty—interspersed with bursts of laughter. Rockford had seated Tory next to Bart Whitaker while he had gone to sit opposite with two other ladies. Tory had wondered about that at the time, but when she saw him watching her, she knew why he had done so. And when she saw how careful he was not to draw attention to what he was doing, to spare her any censure, she felt warm and grateful for his care.

After a delicious picnic that concluded with champagne and fruit tarts, they joined another group wandering through the rose garden. Rockford picked a white rosebud and kissed it before he gave it to her. Once again it was done so quickly and so gracefully, no one noticed. Tory blushed a little as she put it in the lace at her bosom.

Eventually they went down to the river, accompanied by Bart Whitaker. Viscount Dorr had also tried to make one of the party, but since Tory only had two sides, he had been forced to take himself off, disconsolate.

"Another conquest, Tory?" Bart teased.

"He is becoming rather tiresome," she said. "But he's a nice young man. I would not give him pain."

"He is a puppy. A brash puppy who should be put in his place," the marquess announced. "The sooner you send him about his business, the better."

Tory did not reply, but Bart Whitaker leaned forward, looking past her profile in some amazement. What he saw on Rockford's face caused his brows to rise, and he was quick to excuse himself.

When Tory and the marquess reached the landing, another couple was just returning a boat. He helped her into it while a boatman held it steady. Then he took his own seat on the center thwart and pushed off.

Tory sat in the stern, watching him. He had removed his coat for greater ease, and she could see his body under the fine linen of his shirt. The muscles in his arms moved smoothly as he stroked, feathered, and returned the oars, and his chest muscles were taut and powerful looking. When she saw he was smiling at her, she pretended she had to adjust her parasol.

"Why are we going so far upstream, sir?" she asked in the sudden silence, dabbling a hand in the cool water. "No one else has done so."

"Because when we decide to return, all I will have to do is relax," he said. "Rivers run to the sea. Besides, there is the tide to consider. It is on the turn now."

They spoke then of where they had lived as children, the games they had liked to play, the names of their first ponies. But when Tory asked about his family, Nick Sinclair's face darkened.

"What is it?" she asked. "What have I said to distress you?"

"My immediate family are all dead," he replied, resting a moment on the oars. "My mother, father, and younger sister were killed in a carriage accident four years ago."

"I am so sorry!" she exclaimed, reaching out to press his hand. "I did not know."

He looked down at that hand clad in its white glove, and wished she were not wearing it, so he could feel her touch more intimately. Then he shrugged. "It was very sad. And a bad way to come into the title. You see, by all rights I should have been with them, but I had stayed an extra day at a friend's estate some miles away. Strange, isn't it, how fate plays a role in our lives?"

"My grandmother would have said your guardian angel was watching over you," Tory told him.

"How unfortunate *their* guardian angels were not on duty," he replied, his mouth twisting a little. After a short pause Tory changed the subject, and she did not mention his family again. She had seen his pain, realized this was a sore spot that he could not bear to have touched, and she was more sorry for him than she could say.

But Nick Sinclair was a pleasant companion that afternoon. No, more than pleasant, Tory decided. He made her feel interesting and intelligent by the questions he asked her, and the careful way he listened to her replies. Gone were the brittle social comments, the sly double entendres of a bored peer, and in his place remained only a sensible, personable man Tory found she was beginning to admire.

And he made her feel beautiful and desirable as well, for she could see the admiration in his eyes, and note the way those eyes lingered on her face, her throat. She told herself it was just as well they were only to be alone together in a tippy rowboat where they could not change their seats lest it capsize.

Eventually they drifted back downriver. Tory wished they could have remained alone longer, but she knew it would not be wise. Why, Anne might be looking for her even now, wondering where she was. And there were so many old gossips who might have noted the length of time she and the marquess had been absent, and who were busy discussing it among themselves. Tory sighed. It was not the way she would have chosen to end this magical afternoon.

At the landing, she saw the crowd had thinned considerably, for some of the guests had already left for town.

"Is it very late?" she asked, a worried frown creasing her brow.

Sinclair reached up a gentle finger to smooth that frown away. "No, not very. Don't worry."

"I was only afraid my cousin might be wondering where I have been," she explained, nervous of him suddenly, as she had not been all afternoon.

He took her arm. "Shall we go and reassure her?" he asked. "And I would ask her to permit me to drive you back to town in my curricle."

"Oh, you mustn't do that," she said quickly. "I could not possibly go with you."

"It's because of your father, isn't it?" he asked stiffly after a long, pregnant pause. "He wouldn't approve, would he? And your mother would be horrified. No doubt they would both be very angry."

Tory stopped and turned to him. "Yes, I am sorry to say, they would be. And I don't want any scenes to mar this wonderful day. Besides, we were only going to pretend while we were here at the fete, weren't we?"

He could not withstand the little pleading he heard in her voice. "Of course, if that is what you wish. But I hope we will find ourselves in accord more often."

Tory nodded, and he went on, "Does that nod mean you are willing to forget my past and my reputation?"

Her clear green eyes studied his rugged face. "I don't know that I can forget it, sir," she said honestly. "Your past and reputation are a part of you. But I can say I will surely think of you differently after today."

She looked around then, and she smiled. "There is Anne now, on the terrace with Bart. I had forgotten they were great friends once upon a time."

"They were?" he asked, intrigued. As far as he knew, Bart Whitaker was not much in the petticoat line. And from their nuncheon together, he had discovered Lady Garen to be a very independent, outspoken woman. He would hardly have thought her Bart's type.

"It was before her marriage," Tory explained. "I remember it well because she came to spend several months with us one year while her parents were traveling abroad. She was sixteen, and I was only six, and a terrible pest. You see, I adored her and followed her everywhere. And I do remember that where Anne was that summer, so was Bart."

"Just the man I wanted to see," that gentleman said as the marquess and Tory joined them. "I came out to the fete with Lord Ames, but since the Countess of Wills coaxed him to take her back to town, I am now in need of a lift myself. Could you possibly take me up, Rockford?"

Before the marquess could speak, Lady Garen said, "No, no, sir! There is no need. You shall come in my carriage with Tory and me. There is plenty of room."

For a moment, Tory was disappointed, for she had thought to discuss the marquess with Anne on the return journey. Now that would be impossible. Still, she could call on her in a day or two. And perhaps it would be better to keep her own counsel while she remembered this day, relived it. It had been unlike any she could recall. Her lips curved in a smile as she remembered how she and Nick Sinclair had laughed together on the river when a mother duck had paddled out of the reeds near the bank, her ducklings in a neat line behind her. But seeing the boat and the two humans in it, Mama Duck had swung about sharply, quacking a warning to her brood as she did so. She had been so comical as she herded them back to the safety of the reeds, both Tory and the marquess had laughed aloud, which only made Mama quack even louder.

Tory looked up to see Nick Sinclair watching her again, his rueful little grin telling her how much he regretted he could not drive her home himself.

When Lady Garen's carriage left a few minutes later, the marquess went to take leave of his hostess.

Lady Carr was delighted he was alone, for she had a number of subtle questions she longed to ask him. But Sinclair was too clever for her. Laughing as he bent to kiss her, he said, "Yes, I know it is very bad of me to run away, but I cannot stay. It was a marvelous party, as yours always are. I thank you for indulging me by giving it."

"Perhaps someday you will tell me why it was so important to have the fete at all," the lady said a little tartly. "Not that I mean to pry, of course."

"Of course not," he agreed so quickly and

smoothly, she rapped his arm with her fan and scolded him as Toby led the team and curricle forward.

The marquess said very little on the return drive, and for once, Toby held his tongue. But every so often he darted a glance at the man sitting beside him, and, seeing his preoccupation, smiled to himself.

Nick Sinclair did not notice. He was recalling the afternoon, and Tory Emerson. What a lovely girl she was, he thought. Her black curls had gleamed in the sunlight, and in her white gown, only those curls and her green eyes and delicate complexion had lent her color. But what glorious color that had been! He had not been able to keep his eyes from her, especially when the light from the river in all its changing patterns had been reflected on her face.

When he recalled the kiss they had shared, he grimaced a little. Her lips had been so sweet, so tentative. Obviously she had never been kissed by a lover before. At the time he had felt a great wave of sadness and regret sweep over him for his lost innocence. Even he had felt no one should touch Victoria Emerson except a man who could come to her as virtuous as she was. But such thoughts were maudlin. He could not help the man he had become, and not even for the glorious Miss Emerson, could he change.

Still, he felt more than a little uneasy remembering what he had set out to do at the beginning of the Season. True, he still wanted to punish her father for his snub, but he wished he could do so in a way that would not punish his daughter as well.

He suspected she was not as indifferent to him as she had once pretended. Perhaps she was even falling in love with him. What a terrible phrase that was! Falling into debt, into trouble, into despair. Falling off a cliff, falling in love—dangerous all. Still, where Miss Emerson was concerned, one forgot that.

Was it because she was so special? Besides her beauty, she was intelligent, and she had a generous soul. How quickly she had tried to comfort him when he had told her about his family! How smoothly she had changed the subject when she saw he did not care to discuss the tragedy. And not once all afternoon had she mentioned his reputation as a rake and a gambler, not even in passing or in jest.

It had been grand to pretend with her. But why did he wish that it had not been just "pretend"?

He was surprised to discover then that he had arrived back in town, without even being aware of the miles he had traveled. He forced himself to put his memories aside so he could concentrate on the crowded streets.

"Did you have a good day, guv?" Toby asked, as if aware he could speak to his master now, without fear of being reprimanded.

"Most enjoyable," the marquess said briefly. Toby grinned.

"I saw you with that Miss Emerson," he confided next. " 'Course I was way over by the stables, but she surely is pretty, isn't she?"

"Outstanding," the marquess agreed, but his voice was colder now.

"Do you like her a lot, guv?" Toby persisted, ignoring that warning signal. "More than that Lucy you kept?"

"I've told you before, my business is not yours, boy," Sinclair snarled, frowning heavily. "This is the last time I'll warn you. Keep your freckled nose out of my affairs, or you'll be sorry for it."

Toby shrugged as his master took a corner at speed. "If you say so, guv. I just thought to ask, you know. No harm in asking, is there?"

The searing sideways glance his master bestowed on him informed him that yes, indeed, there was a great deal of harm in that pursuit; wisely Toby questioned him no more.

Tory Emerson called on her cousin the afternoon following the fete. She was so confused that she felt she needed guidance, and she most certainly could not ask her Mama nor the clinging Miss Essex for that, not when it concerned the Marquess of Rockford!

But after his kiss yesterday, all the golden afternoon they had spent together, she had begun to wonder if it were possible Nicholas Sinclair was truly smitten. He had certainly acted that way. Remembering the rosebud he had given her, which was now safely hidden in her prayer book, Tory blushed.

But he could only be playing some deep game to amuse himself during the Season. She would ask Anne. She would know, better than someone newly come to town, even if she were one and twenty.

After a spirited discussion with her old governess, Tory went to her cousin's alone.

"Indeed, dear Anne, sometimes I think I will lose my mind if she does not let me alone," she said.

Lady Garen noticed her flashing eyes and chuckled. "It is unfortunate you are burdened so, but as soon as you marry, all this being hedged about will be a thing of the past."

"Marry? *You* are suggesting I marry? You?" Tory

teased, forgetting her gloomy old governess immediately, as Anne had intended.

"It is the only way you will be able to gain any freedom at all, for when you have a husband, you will not need either your mother, your father, or Miss Essex."

"But I will have a husband instead," Tory reminded her. "Where is the difference?"

"Oh, husbands are nowhere near as confining and fussy as parents and elderly companions who have known you since you were in pinafores. After the first month or so, you will be able to do exactly as you please. And properly handled, a husband will be only too agreeable to returning to his own pursuits, while allowing you to get on with yours."

"That does not sound very loving, or exciting," Tory said slowly.

Her cousin smiled a little. "I forgot you must think of marriage that way. Most young girls do. But do rid your mind of any such illusions, for most marriages are not exciting in the least. After the honeymoon they become, at the most, comfortable arrangements, more habit than delight."

Tory mulled over her cousin's remarks as the tea tray was brought in, and Anne busied herself with it. She did so hope Anne's views of matrimony were not true. She wanted to love her husband, and she certainly wanted him to love her. Madly. And forever.

Recalled to her original purpose in visiting, she wondered how she could introduce the subject of the Marquess of Rockford. Before she could do so, however, the butler announced Miss Deering.

Tory had met this particular friend of her cousin's before and liked her very much, but today she had to hide impatience at the interruption.

Phoebe Deering was a thin woman in her forties. She had never married, and did not seem to regret it. Now she came in, kissed Lady Garen, waved merrily to Tory, and took the chair the butler had drawn up for her.

"I do hope you are admiring my entrance, ladies," she said as she accepted the cup Anne gave her. "Just in time for tea, and I see cook has made my favorite muffins. What could be better?

"But before I forget it, here is the book I told you about, Anne. You must tell me what you think of it, and its author. She may call herself 'an unknown lady,' but I have my suspicions. I'll be surprised if you don't agree with me.

"Miss Emerson, you are looking as lovely as always. That shade of blue becomes you."

Tory thanked her as Anne went to put the book safely away. Miss Deering never failed to pay her a compliment, which she enjoyed even though it was obvious the lady herself cared nothing for appearances. Today, for example, she was wearing a bonnet trimmed with limp, faded roses, her puce gown was creased, and the flounce at the hem was coming undone.

"Have you heard the news?" Miss Deering asked as she took two muffins from the plate Tory held out to her. "I have just now come from Lady Waring's where everything is confusion and grief."

"I have not been out today," Anne Garen admitted.

"The news has just reached town. And Althea Waring heard it first because she is the poor young man's aunt. Such weeping and wailing and wringing of hands! But one can hardly blame her. It is too bad, much too bad."

"Phoebe, do stop beating around the bush and

tell us this news," Lady Garen said severely. "If you do not, I shall remove the muffins."

"I was just about to, and I am through with the muffins anyway," her friend said with dignity. "Word has come that Randolph Sperling shot himself a few nights ago. He left a note saying he could not repay his gambling debts, and so there was no other recourse for him but suicide. Lady Waring is devastated, for young Randolph was the last of his line, and what is left of the estates must go to distant cousins. She is even now making preparations to go into the country to be with her sister for the funeral."

"Randolph Sperling," Anne Garen said slowly as she stirred her tea. Across from her, Tory Emerson looked from one lady to the other in bewilderment. She did not know a Mr. Sperling. At least she couldn't remember being introduced to anyone of that name.

"Ah, yes, I do know of him," Anne Garen went on. "Recently I heard tales of his bad luck at the tables. Wasn't he in debt to the Marquess of Rockford?"

As Tory hid a gasp, Miss Deering nodded. "Yes, deeply dipped, from all accounts. Gambling! It is so horrid! Imagine wagering away your fortune, your lands, even your ancestral home! And how could Rockford continue to play with the poor man—take more and more of his money? He must have known his desperate circumstances, don't you think? Men! They are incomprehensible to me, and always have been."

"But you must remember women too can be addicted to gambling," Anne Garen reminded her.

Tory sat quietly as the two friends continued to discuss the unhappy news. If what she had just learned was true, Nicholas Sinclair had, in effect, been responsible for young Sperling's death. How terrible for him! What must he be feeling now, knowing that because of him, a friend had been so despairing and impoverished, he had felt his only way out was to put a pistol to his head and pull the trigger. Surely after such a tragedy, the marquess would never gamble again. Not that that would help poor Mr. Sperling and his grieving family, though.

And then she caught herself up sharply. What on earth was she thinking? Pitying Rockford because *he* might be remorseful? Dear Lord in heaven, he did not deserve pity. This horrible state of affairs had come about because of him. And this was the man she had allowed to kiss her yesterday? This was the monster she had smiled at and laughed with, whose rosebud she had held to her cheek last night—the man she'd dreamed about?

Her cup clattered a little as she put it down, and her cousin looked up quickly. Seeing how white Tory had become, how wide and fixed her eyes, she turned to her friend and frowned a warning. Phoebe Deering immediately changed the subject, scolding herself for not remembering how young and naive Anne's cousin was. She shouldn't have mentioned the suicide in her presence, and she was sorry she had done so.

Not, she told herself as she chattered away of the play she had seen the evening before, that she was an advocate of hiding the truth from young girls. In her opinion, the sooner they learned how unpleasant life could be on occasion, the better for them.

Ten

NICK SINCLAIR HAD heard the news earlier in the day when he visited White's. The entire club was ahum with it, and a few elderly members looked at him sternly as he passed. The marquess ignored them. True, he regretted Sperling's death, but mostly he was horrified to discover that a man he had always considered rational and capable, had been a coward. For to Nick Sinclair, the act of taking your life did not show courage or great resolution. Rather it showed you could not face the consequences of your actions; you could not cope. And so you ran away. To death, as it happened in this case.

He told himself he had nothing to be ashamed of. Indeed, a number of his acquaintances reassured him on that point. And when Mr. Marmaduke Ainsworth was asked by another gentleman if he intended to continue to associate with Rockford, Duke had stared at him, completely astounded.

"Why ever not, man?" he had asked brusquely. "Surely it wasn't Sinclair's fault Sperling gambled his fortune away. Couldn't have stopped him, y'know. Determined to go to hell in a handbasket, from what I could see. And if it hadn't been Sinclair, it would have been someone else. You, maybe."

The man had recoiled and hurried away, and Ainsworth had gone to seek out the marquess to assure him of his continued esteem.

"Thank you, Duke," Nick said seriously. "Amazing, isn't it? Somehow because Sperling took the easy way out, I am to be held accountable."

"Not by many. Only by a few idiots, y'know."

Over Ainsworth's shoulder, the marquess could see that Mr. Gerald Emerson had arrived and was deep in conversation with two other middle-aged men. He was sure they were regaling him with the latest *on-dit*, and when Emerson looked up and saw him watching him, then colored up and turned away once again, Nick was sure of it.

Glancing over his own shoulder, Duke chuckled. "I see you have not endeared yourself to the proper Mr. Emerson yet. But never tell me you are enamored of his daughter."

"Of course not," Sinclair said promptly, and wondered if he lied.

"Still, she is a beauty, no denying that," Duke said as the two sat down at a table and the marquess raised his hand to summon a footman. "It's plain to see others are smitten. Why, Quentin is in a fair way of making a cake of himself. And then there's Lord Dorr. Glad to hear you at least have retained your sanity, dear boy. At the rate my other friends are succumbing to matrimony, I'll not have a single unwed crony to m'name."

The marquess smiled, but said no more, for an arresting picture of himself and Miss Emerson in the marriage bed had invaded his mind. Shaking himself mentally, he ordered wine.

As the footman hurried away, however, he suddenly wished he had not. Instead, he wanted to leave the club with all its whispering gentlemen—

the knowing looks, even those of commiseration and support. But he knew that to do so would be fatal, for it would tell everyone he felt more than remorse over Sperling's death. It would tell them he felt guilt, and that would never do, he told himself as he took the glass the footman presented.

"Have you heard anymore of the suicide, Duke?" he asked instead.

"Only that he did try to find the money, but there wasn't enough. He'd already mortgaged everything that wasn't entailed. Those cousins who inherit now will not be pleased with the state of affairs, I'm afraid. Pity, that. I was at Sperling Hall once. A noble estate, been in the family since Henry the Eighth."

He shook his head. "Now it's nothing but bits and pieces, and the hall itself is falling down stone by stone from neglect.

"Ah, there's Bart just arrived! Forgive me if I leave you. I've something to discuss with him."

Sinclair waved a careless hand. He was sure someone else would be only too eager to take Ainsworth's vacated chair in hope of gleaning some gossip of the suicide unknown to the rest. Although why they thought he would know anything out of the ordinary, escaped him. Cynically he watched two men hurry toward him.

That evening, after a solitary dinner, he decided he must go out again. Putting off the inevitable would only make it more difficult later. And it was better to get the ladies' reaction to the scandal over and done with as quickly as possible. There would be no hurried trip out of town for him this time. It was too serious.

As he rose from the table, he wondered how Victoria Emerson would take the news. She did not look kindly on gambling; why, only consider how she had taken him to task about it once, that morning they had met on horseback in Hyde Park.

He was to discover in short order. After presenting his card of invitation at Lord Carleton's in Hanover Square, and greeting his host, Nick Sinclair strolled into one of the drawing rooms. It was crowded of course, for the Season was in full bloom, and the ton was out in force. Did he just imagine the little lull in conversation when he entered, or was it possible he was becoming too sensitive?

He bowed to Lady Jersey when she shook her finger at him and sighed. Smiling, he moved on. Mrs. Jackson demanded his attention, and since she was an old favorite of his, he lingered beside her. But when at last she let him go after a mighty scold, none the less effective for being delivered in a hoarse whisper, he saw Victoria Emerson across the room. She was surrounded by her usual court. This time it included two young ladies, who no doubt had seen the wisdom of remaining nearby. For when Miss Emerson's hand was claimed for a set, the other gentlemen would be forced to look elsewhere, and they would be right at hand. Intelligent girls, Nick thought as he made his slow way across the room. When he reached the group, he saw to his surprise Miss Emerson was nowhere in sight. Her late companions were already beginning to disperse, Lord Dorr looking especially forlorn, Nick thought as he turned to search the room.

A piece of a sprigged muslin skirt just whisking out the door caught his eye. It looked very much like part of the dress Victoria Emerson was wearing, and he started back the way he had come, determined to follow her. Later, he could not recall a more frustrating evening. True, he was often detained by people eager to discuss the tragedy with him, but even so, the lady he sought remained unaccessible. Finally, after following her from the red drawing room to the hall, and thence to the library and on to the blue and gold drawing room, and never getting any closer to her, he was forced to admit Victoria Emerson was deliberately avoiding him.

His face stiffened into a ferocious frown, and a young lady who had been sent over to him by her ever-hopeful mother stopped abruptly, about-faced, and hurried away.

Thoroughly incensed, Nick Sinclair made his way to the terrace. There were others there, so he moved to the far end where he could be alone. How dare she do this? he asked himself. How dare she avoid him, especially after the wonderful afternoon they had spent together at the fete? But perhaps she was only acting on her father's orders? He told himself that must be it. But eventually, when all the chatter died down, when the ton had some juicy new scandal to discuss, Miss Emerson was sure to relent, and then we shall see. Oh, yes, Miss Victoria Emerson, then indeed we shall see, he told himself grimly.

He remained on the terrace for a long time, leaning against the balustrade and staring down into the dark garden beyond while he smoked one of the thin cigars he occasionally enjoyed. Behind him, the noise of the party was easily ignored. The night breeze cooled his face, and he felt his anger begin to slip away.

And then he heard her laugh, that gay, musical sound he had remarked at first meeting, and he turned quickly. She was with Lord Dorr, and although there were a few other couples scattered here and there about the terrace, those two were alone. Obviously Miss Emerson thought he had left the party, gone home in a rage, no doubt, and had decided it was now perfectly safe to venture out in the dark. With that idiot Dorr, as well, the marquess thought as he threw his cigar away, and started toward them.

He saw the young viscount put his hands on her arms and caress them while he spoke to her earnestly.

As he neared them, he heard her say, "Come now, sir, I have told you I do not care for fulsome compliments, nor do I care to be manipulated like this. I wonder where Miss Ford and Sir Angus are? I was sure they were to join us here, were they not?"

"Miss Emerson! Victoria! You must let me speak! I adore you, no, I love you more than life itself! You must allow me to call on your father and beg your hand in marriage! Say you will permit me to do that! Say it!"

She put her hands on his chest and pushed, for in his ardor, Lord Dorr had clasped her in his arms. "Please, sir, people are sure to notice," she said, her voice a little annoyed.

"I will let you go when you give me permission to speak to your father," he declared, made bold by the exciting armful he held.

"You will let me go at once," she insisted.

"I believe you heard the lady, m'lord," Rockford said in a voice that dripped icicles. It would be hard to say whose gasp was more pronounced, the hapless Lord Dorr or the startled Victoria Emerson.

"You!" she exclaimed.

He bowed before he faced the viscount again. "We

will excuse you, sir. Obviously the lady does not look kindly on your suit. My condolences."

"Well, here now, I say," Lord Dorr sputtered. "Who are you to, I mean, by what right do you, that is . . ."

"Oh, do go away and stop being so tiresome," Tory said in an angry undertone, for she had seen the heads turning their way and knew they had some very interested witnesses.

The viscount seemed stunned by her directive. He bowed, mumbled something, and departed. Nick Sinclair turned back to Tory Emerson to see her eyes were flashing fire.

"You!" she said again. "You can go away as well, sir. I do not care to talk to you."

"Whether you do or not, you will," he said, his grim voice at odds with his pleasant smile as he acknowledged a couple nearby. "We will go to the other end of the terrace. We seem to be attracting some unwanted attention here, thanks to that panting puppy you insist on encouraging."

Tory bit back an angry denial, and preserved instead a dignified silence. Her mind was working frantically as she pondered how she was to handle this man she had hoped to avoid. Perhaps if she excused herself? But somehow she was sure he would not let her go. Even if she tried to make a run for it, she thought him quite capable of physically detaining her. And how people would talk then! Besides, and to be honest with herself, after their rapport at the garden party, Tory felt she owed him an explanation. She resigned herself to a most unpleasant next few minutes.

"Perhaps you will be so good as to tell me why you have been playing at hide-and-seek with me this evening, ma'am?" he asked, getting right to the heart of the matter. "Did you do so at your father's express orders? I notice he accompanied you to the party, and I know he has warned you away from me, dangerous rake that I am. Be truthful now, hasn't he?"

"Yes, but he did that weeks ago," she said. "And yes, I have been avoiding you, but that was because I wanted to, not from any order my father might have given me."

She paused and took a deep breath before she added, "You see, I have discovered you are not a man I want to know, and most certainly don't want to have as a friend. I prefer not to see you or talk to you again."

He stopped then and turned to her to put his hands on her arms, much as Lord Dorr had done. Tory discovered she could not avoid his eyes. They burned down into hers, and she realized he was furious. Strangely she was not afraid. She was only very, very sad.

"So you are going to blame me for Sperling's suicide, too, are you? I thought you too intelligent for that," he said grimly.

"People are staring at us still," she replied.

He looked around, saw the truth of her words and released her, but only to take her arm and lead her to a marble bench set in an alcove nearby. A large urn filled with spring flowers gave them some privacy.

"What did you mean, you thought I was too intelligent to blame you?" she demanded as he put his hands on her shoulders and pressed until she was forced to sit down.

As he took the seat beside her, he said, "What do you think I could possibly have had to do with Sperling's death? He was miles away from London at Sperling Hall. I was not there. I did not load his pistol. I did not aim or fire it. I did not even goad him to the act, indeed, I . . ."

"Do not insult the intelligence you have just been complimenting by quibbling, sir! Of course you were not *directly* involved. But in effect you did goad him into it. By continuing to play with him when you knew he was deep in debt, and knew as well how impossible it was for him to make a recovery, you signed his death certificate."

"I had no idea of the state of his finances," came the swift reply. "It is not something gentlemen demand to know about each other before they sit down at the table. One assumes a man will not play if he cannot pay his losses. But since you are so interested, Miss Emerson, I will tell you I did try to keep him from playing. He would not have it, however. It is often that way. Once men lose badly, they try to recoup their losses by playing again with the man who holds their vowels. It is considered bad form for that man to refuse them the opportunity. So you see, there was nothing I could do."

"Oh, yes, there was, but you did not avail yourself of it lest you look cheap," Tory told him, her voice shaking a little. "Bad form, indeed! And because of this ridiculous *code* men have, Mr. Sperling lost his life."

"He *took* his life, he did not lose it. And it was a cowardly thing he did."

Tory gazed at his grim face in horror. "And that is all you have to say, sir? That he was a *coward*? You have no regrets, no . . ."

"Of course I regret what happened! I am not a monster! Do try to see my side of it, if you can forget your moral sermonizing for a moment, that is.

"Can you imagine what it is like to be blamed for something you had nothing to do with? And had no way of preventing? Yes, Randolph Sperling is dead, and I do regret that death. But I am not to blame for it!"

"Have you ever considered that if you had not gambled even once in your life, Mr. Sperling might still have his?"

He put his head in his hands for a moment as if to clear it. When he lowered them and stared at her, Tory almost cried out. He looked so despairing, so lost, she had to swallow hard lest the tears she could feel coming filled her eyes and he would discover how much all this mattered to her, and wonder why.

"No, I had not thought of that," he said in an emotionless voice. "I don't believe it, though. If it had not been I who won his money, it would have been someone else. Sperling was addicted. Gambling was in his blood. He could not stop."

"As you cannot stop," she said just as softly. "Isn't that so, sir? Aren't you two of a kind?"

Out of the corner of his eye, the marquess saw Gerald Emerson approaching, his step hurried and his face almost purple with anger. Still, he did not rush into speech, try to deny the truth of what she had just said. He did not do so because he was not at all sure she wasn't right. It was true he had not gamed lately, but wasn't that because of his dearth of partners? As soon as his luck changed, and he began to lose along with everyone else, wouldn't he return to his former ways? He did not know.

"I imagine you are right, Miss Emerson," he said, just as her father halted before them, trying to control his breathing.

"Papa," Tory exclaimed, getting to her feet, her

lovely face full of concern. "Are you all right? You do not look at all well."

"Come, Victoria," her father managed to gasp. "It is late. Time we went home."

"Of course," she agreed, patting his arm as she studied his face. Completely ignoring the marquess, Mr. Emerson hustled her away to the doors to the drawing room.

"Servant, Miss Emerson, sir," Nick Sinclair murmured to their retreating backs. He felt a pain in the vicinity of his heart. He had not been so depressed since his family's untimely deaths. He was not even tempted to smile when he thought of the lecture Victoria Emerson was about to receive from her doting parents. Her father, especially, was sure to rage at her for being on a dark terrace with a man he not only abhorred but had expressly warned her to have nothing to do with.

He went to the balustrade again and leaned against it. As he did so, he wondered if he should now put paid to the original snub Gerald Emerson had given him. This evening's snub would have to go unpunished, for there was small chance he would ever be alone with Victoria Emerson again.

He was surprised that contemplating their coming separation could make him feel so grim.

Eleven

THE DRIVE BACK to South Audley Street was accomplished in a leaden silence broken only by the tiny sobs Mrs. Emerson could not quite stifle in her handkerchief. Tory sat quietly beside her mother, not bothering to ask why they had left the party so suddenly. She did not care for the way her father was glaring at her, or his heightened complexion. He looked like a man on the verge of apoplexy.

Mr. Emerson directed the butler to send the servants to bed and take himself off with them, before he pushed Tory into the library. Her mother trailed after her, making distressed little noises still, and Mr. Emerson shut the doors behind them all with a resounding click.

"Now, miss, we'll have the whole tale of this night's work without further ado," he began, throwing down his gloves and cane before settling himself heavily behind his desk. "Sit there," he ordered, pointing to the chair that fronted the desk.

"Papa, I do not understand what has upset you so," Tory began as she obeyed him. "I know you don't care for the Marquess of Rockford, but surely . . ."

"Care?" he snarled. "I loathe the man and all he stands for! And I have made my sentiments clear

many a time, indeed, ordered you to stay away from him ..."

"I beg your pardon, sir, but that you did not do," Tory dared to say. Her mother moaned softly in her distress, but she ignored her. "You only warned me of him, his reputation and his gambling. And I listened to you, indeed I did."

Mr. Emerson rose suddenly to lean over his desk. He towered above her, red-faced and wild-eyed. "It was not necessary for me to give you an order, miss! My repugnance for the man should have been enough to make you shun him. Yet you deliberately sought him out. Encouraged him, even. Why?"

"Sought him out?" she echoed. "Oh, no, I did not do that. I have been introduced to him, yes, and talked to him on a few occasions, for he is invited everywhere, you know. But I never sought him out or encouraged him."

"How came you to be alone with him tonight, then, far from the rest of the party? I'll have a straight answer now!"

He did not wait for her reply, but rushed on, "Why did you allow him to snatch you away from Lord Dorr's escort? Why didn't you cut him, and return to the drawing room?"

Tory's eyes widened. "But to do so would have caused all kinds of comment. The terrace was crowded. People were staring, partly because ..."

"I've no doubt they were staring, no doubt at all! My, yes! The sight of a young miss in her first season being so depraved as to encourage the worst rake in the realm would be enough to make anyone stare!" her father said sarcastically.

"How do you know this, Papa?" Tory asked.

"Lord Dorr came and told me. He seems a nice fellow, thinks just as he ought. And I was grateful for his warning. Heaven knows what would have happened if I had not come to get you, since I discover you are dead to all proper feeling."

Tory bit back a heated reply. She must stay calm, she must.

"I have heard other distressing news, miss," he went on. "A Mrs. Hawley spoke to your mother tonight about your behavior at Lady Carr's garden party."

Tory's heart began to pound, but she only said, "Who is Mrs. Hawley? I do not believe I have met her."

"No doubt. She is barely known to your mother, but she is, I gather, a woman who does not miss a thing."

"And she tells everyone what she sees, everyone! She is London's prime tattler," Mrs. Emerson contributed. "Oh, dear, it is so very unfortunate . . ."

Her husband spared her a searing glance, and she subsided in her handkerchief again.

"That is immaterial. What is important is that she says you spent the entire party in Rockford's company, even going so far as to disappear on the river with him for hours. Well, miss, what have you to say to that?"

Tory did not flinch. "It is true I saw the marquess there, but we were not alone except for the brief time, when he took me out in a rowboat on the Thames. We were not gone 'for hours,' Papa, how absurd! As if Anne would ever countenance such a thing, even if I were so lost to all decency as to agree to it. Mrs. Hawley is nothing but a troublemaker."

"Be silent!" Gerald Emerson bellowed, causing his wife to cry out, and Tory to recoil in her chair. Never had her father raised his voice to her like that, never. She was more than shocked, she was appalled, and for the first time she began to fear him a little. Surely he would not hit her, would he? She kept her eyes from the slim cane he had used this evening, and tried to look at ease.

"I'll hear no more of your 'explanations,' miss!" he said. "Weaving your deceitful words, trying to take me in, or so you think. But I am not a green young man, and I understand you very well. As you will discover, things are going to be very different from now on. There will be no more gadding about with only a maid or a footman to trail you, no, indeed. No more parties for you, unless you go to them with both your mother and me."

"But, Papa," Tory said as he paused to take a breath, "have you forgotten that I am one and twenty? Much too old for such chaperonage?" A picture of her life in London from now on flashed through her mind, and she had to hide a shudder.

"Ha! You may be one and twenty, but you haven't the sense of a hen. And as far as being able to discern good from evil, even less than that.

"Well, you are not going to see Anne Garen again except on a few, formal occasions. I ken well her influence over a previously well-behaved, docile daughter has been disastrous. And when you do see her, both your mother and Miss Essex will be with you. Furthermore, you are not to leave this house without both of them in attendance. You are not to be trusted!

"Whether you will ever have more freedom again, will depend entirely on your future behavior. Be warned, however, I shall not relent or be moved by tears or supplication until I am sure you have learned your lesson.

"Go to bed. I have nothing more to say to you."

Tory stood up. She was upset, furious, unrepentant, but she made herself go to him for a good-night kiss. When he only pointed sternly to the door, she realized she had angered him as she had never done before.

As she went up the stairs to bed, she wondered how she was to survive her imprisonment. To think she must be constantly in Essie's and her mother's company sank her spirits. And to know she would be watched ceaselessly by her father at any party she was allowed to attend, was too depressing to contemplate.

She cried a little as she removed her evening gown. Still, had what she done been dire enough to warrant such a withdrawal of their affection? After all, she had not been indiscreet, and what did it matter if her father did not care for Rockford? She did not care for him herself anymore, and after this evening had planned to have nothing more to do with him.

Climbing into bed at last, Tory wondered why she had not thought to tell that to her father. Surely it would have eased his mind. But after the way he had treated her, somehow she felt he did not deserve such consideration.

A week later, Tory was still confined in her luxurious prison. Waited on, pampered, but confined. True, she had been allowed to go on a shopping expedition with her mother and Essie, and her father had indulged her once with a drive in the park at the fashionable hour of five o'clock. She had seen a few of her acquaintances there, but nothing of the Marquess of Rockford. Which was just as well, she decided as Gerald Emerson instructed the coachman to return to South Audley Street. Papa had not wavered in his decision to keep her close, and the only gentleman he had had the carriage stopped for had been Viscount Dorr.

Tory had also attended a soiree and two receptions, as well as a concert of sacred music, at all times hemmed in on either side by her parents. Bart Whitaker had come to speak to her at the soiree to beg a dance, only to be told Miss Emerson was not dancing that evening. He had bowed and gone away, but not before he had sent a questioning glance to Tory, who dared not, even by the slightest sign, communicate her trouble to him. Still, she suspected he would understand. Bart was a clever man, and her father's hovering, his stern frowns and constant looking about as if to discover some danger only he could see, made the situation obvious. She told herself if she had not been involved, she would have laughed at her father, for the situation was ludicrous, and he was behaving as if he were in a bad farce.

Anne came to call one morning a few days later. Since she was a relative, she had to be admitted no matter how Gerald Emerson might disapprove of her, but the visit could not be said to be a success. Not only did Mrs. Emerson and Miss Essex remain in the room the entire time, Mr. Emerson came in at the end of it to glower at her.

"You are not feeling well, sir?" Anne Garen asked coolly. "You look positively bilious."

"My health is fine. But I must tell you, Victoria is not going about as often as she has done before," he said sternly. "You seem to have had a detrimental influence on my little girl. She has been doing too much and is feeling pulled."

"She is hardly a little girl anymore, Uncle. She is

a woman grown. And I fail to see any sign of exhaustion. Indeed, she has seldom looked better."

"That is because she has been kept at home for over a week," came the quick reply.

"Indeed, my dear niece, it has been most kind of you to oblige Victoria, but really, we would prefer you do not," Mrs. Emerson volunteered. "Besides, you have your own friends, your own interests, and we would not impose."

Lady Garen opened her mouth to speak, but Gerald Emerson held up a deterring hand. "No, do not deny the truth of Mrs. Emerson's words. And since my business in town is almost concluded, I shall be supervising Victoria's amusements myself. Where her father is, there is no need for anyone else. Soon we will be returning to the country, moreover, the Season being well advanced."

This was said in such a way as to leave no doubt the gentleman wished they had never left that location and would be more than happy to return to it. Furthermore, he had no intention of ever allowing his precious Victoria to be seduced by London society again. Tory felt only the utmost despair at his words, Anne Garen looked stunned, and only Miss Essex smiled and nodded in complete agreement.

Anne rose to leave shortly after this daunting speech. She shook hands with the governess, kissed her aunt, and came to draw Tory into her arms. As the two hugged, she murmured, "This will work out, whatever it is. But whatever *did* you do?"

Tory could not reply, for Mr. Emerson was there to usher Lady Garen to the hall; he shut the door to the morning room firmly behind him before he did so.

That afternoon, Tory escaped to the garden, a small side yard completely enclosed by a high brick wall to separate it from South Audley Street and the mews, as well as the house next door. The garden had a few wicker chairs set beneath a wide-spreading tree and a curving brick path that was edged with spring flowers. Because there was no way to enter or leave the garden except through the house, Tory had been allowed to use it whenever she wished. Today she hoped she would be able to be solitary for a long time, for Miss Essex had retired with the headache after nuncheon, and Mrs. Emerson was entertaining some friends of hers with an afternoon of silver loo in the drawing room. Her husband had gone to the city to see his man of business.

Tory sighed as she opened her sewing basket. She was feeling almost overcome by the punishment she was still suffering. It was true her father kissed her good night now, as did her mother, and he/ seemed to have lost the towering rage he had shown the night he had discovered her with Nicholas Sinclair, but he had not relaxed his vigilance over her activities, nor had he allowed her an iota of freedom or independence. And now he had sent Anne away! How was she to bear it? she wondered.

"Er, beg your pardon, miss, may I speak to you?" a high, light voice inquired.

Startled, Tory spun around to see the Marquess of Rockford's tiger standing on the garden path, cap in hand.

"However did you get in here?" she asked, her heart pounding at the fright he had given her.

"Came in the back way, I did," Toby said, waving vaguely in the direction of the kitchen.

"You should not be here," Tory scolded. "It could get me in a lot of trouble. And what do you want with me, anyway?"

Had the marquess sent him? she wondered. Was it possible he had a letter for her? A message?

"Don't you worry, miss," Toby said with his wide grin. "No one will know, I promise. I'm here, because well, I had to come. My master, he's been some upset ever since the night he went to that party in Hanover Square."

"Did *he* send you?" Tory asked softly.

The boy shook his head, and she added, "Is he ill?"

"Not in his body, like. But I know he's heartsore."

Tory's own heart began to beat faster. "I don't know what this has to do with me," she protested.

Instead of answering right away, the boy came to settle down on the grass at her feet, without so much as a by-your-leave. Tory was so bemused she did not scold him, as she would have any other servant.

Looking up at her earnestly, he said, "Don't you like him, then, miss? I was so sure you must."

"Well, yes, there have been times when I liked him very well," Tory admitted. "But I do not approve of him; his pastimes or his behavior."

"I know," Toby said wisely. "He has been a bad one. But he's changed, y'know. For one thing he doesn't gamble anymore, and he turned that Lucy away some time ago."

Tory had a very good idea who "Lucy" might be, so she ignored that remark. "Yes, but he was responsible for a man's death, no matter what he says," she persisted.

"Maybe," came the quick reply. "True, he held Sperling's vowels, but I think it could have been anyone. Real gamblers never stop. They play and play until they're ruined."

"Exactly why my father dislikes the marquess so

much," Tory said, then wondered if she were losing her mind to be confiding so much to a servant. Rockford's servant, at that. But there was something about the boy's freckled face, his wide grin, that made her smile broadly in return. Or maybe she spoke freely because he had such honest eyes, and his concern for his master was endearing.

Still she continued to protest: "My father says ..."

"Begging your pardon and no offense meant nor taken I hope, but your father doesn't know *everything*. No one on earth knows *everything*, miss. And isn't it true he wouldn't like any man who loved you? Hasn't he kept you away from men all these years?"

Tory nodded, biting her lower lip as she did so. Gerald Emerson had certainly done that.

"And Nick Sinclair isn't a *real* gambler, miss," Toby went on. "Oh, he's played deep many and many a time, but he never played much at all until his family was killed in that carriage accident four years ago. See, he misses them still. He always will, all his life. And he feels guilty, somehow, as if it's his fault he wasn't killed, too. It weighs on him, it does. And now he has no one at all—no family and no real friends. He's put a glass wall around himself, see, and he won't let anyone in. You know why he does that?"

"No, why?" Tory whispered.

"Because inside he feels if he never loves anyone or lets anyone get close to him, he can't be hurt again. At least he *used* to feel that way."

"But now?" Tory asked, leaning forward a little.

"Now he's met you, miss," Toby told her with his wide grin.

Tory sat back, stunned, and he hurried on, "See, he does like you, and it frightens him. Still, since your father is so angry with him, he knows he can't call on you or send flowers or a letter or anything. But he'd *like* to."

"How do you know these things?" Tory demanded. "Has the marquess spoken to you? Are you sure he didn't send you here to see me, try to persuade me to his side?"

"Oh, no, miss," Toby exclaimed, looking horrified. "He'd have the hide off me if he knew I'd been here. Please don't ever tell him! Not ever! He's never said a word to me about you. In fact, when I've asked if he liked you, he told me it was none of my business. Well, no, I guess it isn't, but *he's* my business, and I want him to be happy. As for how I know, well, just from watching him, listening to him speak, hearing from his valet about how he sits alone in the library late at night just staring into the fireplace. And drinking, too," he added, as if determined to be honest.

"I'm sorry to hear that, but I don't see what I can do. My father never lets me out of his sight anymore."

"I think that might change very soon, miss," Toby said. "And when it does, you'll have to be the one to speak to my master first."

"Oh, I couldn't do that," Tory protested. "Ladies don't do such things, but perhaps you didn't know that. No, if there is to be any communication between us, the marquess will have to make the first move."

Toby snorted as he rose to his feet and dusted off the seat of his livery. "Lots of things ladies don't do, from what I can see. And lots of things they *do* do, they shouldn't. But forget that now. Please, miss, won't you speak to the marquess when you get the chance? Give him some hope-like?"

Tory was not proof against his earnest, pleading gaze. "We'll see," she said. "Maybe."

"Victoria is in the garden? I shall join her. She should not be alone. Bring tea."

Tory turned toward the sound of Essie's voice coming nearer as she walked through the drawing room to the french doors to the garden. Obviously she had vanquished her headache. She turned back then to warn Rockford's lad that he must be off, to discover he was nowhere in sight. Strange that, she thought, as she took out her embroidery and hastily set to work. Of course, she was relieved he had gone before her old governess appeared and demanded an explanation, but where on earth could he have disappeared to so fast?

Twelve

EVERYTHING TOBY HAD told Victoria Emerson about the Marquess of Rockford's moodiness had been true. Sinclair had stopped going to most of the parties he was invited to, and sometimes he did not leave his house all day. His servants were concerned, but only Toby had thought to do something about it by enlisting Victoria Emerson's help.

Only a day after his tiger's invasion of the Emerson garden, Nick Sinclair had a visitor. For a week he had refused to see any callers, but now he told his butler to admit Bartholomew Whitaker. Perhaps I am growing tired of my own company, he sneered at himself as the two men settled down in the library on either side of the fireplace.

"There was some reason you have called, Whitaker?" his host asked. "Not that I am not always delighted to see you, of course."

Whitaker smiled. "No particular reason, unless my little curiosity about Tory Emerson counts as one."

"Yes?" the marquess prompted in a voice that in anyone else would have showed considerable boredom. Bart Whitaker was not misled.

"I've not seen you lately at any parties, and I seldom see Tory, either. And when she is present, her father never leaves her side. Indeed, from the way he hovers over her, you'd think she was in danger of being kidnapped by highwaymen or some other scoundrels."

Nick Sinclair sat up a little straighter, for the germ of an idea was beginning to form in his fertile brain.

"Indeed?" he said. "But you yourself have told me Mr. Emerson has always been most protective of his only child. I fail to see why this behavior is out of the common way."

Bart shook his head. "No, you're wrong there. It is. The other evening I asked Tory for a set and was told by her father that she was not dancing. One has to wonder why. She always does, as you know. And the look she gave me as I excused myself, was so carefully expressionless, it spoke volumes."

Rockford thought for a moment, then he said, "Can I confide in you, sir? Tell you something that must remain between us and never be spoken of outside this room?"

"Of course. I would be honored, and you have my word."

"The story I am about to tell you does not show me in a very good light," Rockford began as he got up quickly to pace the room. "You see, when you first introduced us, I thought Miss Emerson only an exceptionally lovely girl. I don't think I would have had a thing to do with her, except her father had the temerity to snub me the first evening I came face-to-face with him. Looked right through me, he did, and turned his back on me. It angered me."

"I am sure it must have done," his guest said, sitting back and crossing one well-booted leg over the other.

"I decided then and there that I would make Ger-

ald Emerson pay for that snub, so I set about courting Miss Emerson. Very discreetly, of course."

"You certainly were that. I never suspected a
thing until the garden party."

"Yes, he was not there, nor was her mother. I
could be more open. But the reason Emerson is
guarding his daughter now like a dog with a meaty
bone is because he found us in conversation together at the Carleton soiree. He'd warned her to
stay away from me, and she had not obeyed him.
Learning this angered him so, he tore her away
from me, snubbed me again, in fact. The family left
the party almost immediately. If what you told me
is true, he has not relaxed his vigilance even now.

"Tell me, Bart, what do you think would happen
if there was suddenly a storm of talk about him
and his oh-so-obvious possessiveness?" Rockford
asked, stopping his pacing to point a finger at his
guest. "And what do you think would happen if the
ton began to laugh at him?"

"I think you have a fiendish mind, Rockford, but
it might very well work," Whitaker said promptly.
"He's proud, is Gerald Emerson. He would hate the
idea he had become a laughingstock. But I must
dislike any scheme that would hurt my old friend
Tory."

"So would I. But this won't hurt *her*. It will only
release her from what must be an onerous imprisonment."

"Very well. How do you propose to go about it?"

Sinclair took his seat again. He leaned forward
as he said, "I haven't been going out, but now I
think it more than time I rejoin society. I shall go
everywhere, and sooner or later the ton will see for
itself the depth of Mr. Emerson's obsession. You'll
see."

"Yes, but there must be some talk about him before, if your plan is to be effective," Whitaker pointed out. "People must already be watching him, whispering about him."

Nick Sinclair grinned. "Of course. I'll just mention the matter to a few people, and we'll see what happens."

"I could do so as well, to help Tory," Whitaker volunteered. "I've never cared for Gerald Emerson much and the way he treats his daughter seems unhealthy to me. I've often thought he'd rather see her fade away and grow into an elderly spinster than give her to another man. Tory's too lovely for that fate.

"Er, who were you thinking of telling?"

"Well, the first person must be Mrs. Albert Hawley, don't you agree? I rather doubt we'll have to exert ourselves at all, once she is pointed in the right direction."

There was a moment of silence in the library as the two men exchanged grins. Then Bart Whitaker burst into hearty laughter. He was joined almost immediately by Nick Sinclair, both men slapping their knees and rocking back and forth in their chairs.

In the hall, the butler smiled to himself at this sign the marquess was regaining his spirits, and he hurried off to tell the other upper servants the good news.

It seemed only the matter of a few days before all London was discussing Gerald Emerson and his strange preoccupation with his daughter. The ladies gladly spread the story, for since the news of Randolph Sperling's suicide had ceased to shock, there hadn't been a single juicy bit of gossip to amuse them. The gentlemen, too, passed the word in their clubs, at Tattersall's and Gentleman Jackson's. As always, there were several people ready to take the tale at face value, embellish it even, but there were many others who scoffed at it and waited to see firsthand its verity.

They did not have to wait long. The Countess of Wills was giving a gala ball that week, and the Emerson family were to attend. Mr. Emerson had chosen the gown his daughter was to wear himself, and he told her that if she behaved herself, he was willing to allow her to dance on occasion. With gentlemen of his choosing, of course.

Tory tried to look properly grateful, although she kenw the men he favored would not be *her* choice. Still, she managed to feel a little excitement as her maid hooked her into a white gown trimmed with silver, for she had not been out for days.

When she came down to join her parents at last, Mrs. Emerson said she had never seen her looking so well, and her father nodded his approval.

But his good nature did not survive for long. Once at the ball, he shepherded his ladies to a small sofa on one side of the ballroom and took up his position next to it, his demeanor fierce when any unsuitable gentleman ventured near. Lord Dorr was welcomed and given the first set with Tory, and Sir Angus was also able to claim one. But Jaspar Howland, the Earl of Castleton, was sent quickly on his way, and two other dashing gentlemen as well.

Tory began to imagine she heard muffled laughter nearby, and she wondered at it. But it was not until the Marquess of Rockford strolled past, paused to subject her to a piercing glance through his quizzing glass, and favored her with a deep reverent bow, that the laughter swelled to open derision.

Tory looked around, bewildered. Everywhere nearby, people were staring at them and laughing. Some tried to cover their mouths, but it was obvious the Emerson family was causing no end of amusement. She felt her father grasp her shoulder, and looked up at him. She gasped as she did so, for he was glaring at Rockford, his face red and indignant. The hand that grasped her shoulder so protectively tightened until she cried out a little with the pain. He released her at once, and then, as if suddenly aware that he was being ridiculed, stiffened. Beside Tory, Mrs. Emerson clutched her vinaigrette and moaned softly.

"Get your things together," Emerson hissed at them. "We are leaving here at once!"

Privately Tory felt that by fleeing the scene they were only adding to the loss of their dignity. How much better it would have been to remain, to face down their adversaries with a cool stare, force them to stop their laughing and whispering. Still, she said nothing as her father propelled her forward, a firm hand in the small of her back. Her mother followed them, skipping a little every now and then in an effort to keep up. As the three traversed the ballroom, the laughter swelled, and Gerald Emerson's face turned an even darker red.

Once again nothing was said in the carriage on the drive home. Tory was glad of that, for she was sure the footman's and the coachman's ears were on the stretch as they tried to find out the reason for a departure that came so swiftly on the heels of their arrival at the ball.

To her regret, she was sent up to bed immediately. She wanted to hear what her father had to say about this evening, and what he intended to do about it. For a bleak moment when she realized his best course might be to remove the family from London immediately, and so avoid a repeat of the evening's disaster, she said a silent prayer that he would not do that. Then she wondered why staying in town mattered to her so much.

But perhaps it was just as well her mother took the brunt of his fury tonight, Tory thought as her maid unhooked her, her eyes big with questions she dare not ask. My, a London Season was certainly opening her eyes to her father's character, Tory decided. Here he seemed to be in a temper more often than not. Of course she had heard him roar before, but always at a servant or a horse. She hoped he would not blame her for what had happened, although she did not see how anyone could even think her at fault. What had *she* done, after all? No, it was all her father's hovering over her, protecting her, that had caused the ton to laugh at them. If only he could be made to see that!

The following morning, when Tory came downstairs, the butler told her her mother wished to see her at once. Mr. Emerson, he added in suitably solemn tones, had left the house.

"Victoria, my love! How glad I am you are belowstairs at last!" her mother cried as she entered the morning room. "Do shut the door firmly behind you, and come and sit close beside me. I suppose there is no keeping it from the servants—and will you tell me how they always know *everything* practically from the first, no matter how much care is taken?—well, one can but try. I have sent Miss Essex on an errand. We will be quite private."

"What has Papa decided to do, ma'am?" Tory asked as she drew a chair up beside her mother's.

"Oh, it was just dreadful! Such palpitations I had last evening! And your father pacing to and fro and ranting and raving like a madman, yes, exactly like a madman, my dear, and for what? It did no good at all, and I finally told him so. We discussed the ball then and what happened, and I suggested that perhaps we had been keeping you too close. He was incensed, of course, and refused to modify his ways. Finally he said we would go home to Devon, and ordered me to start packing today."

"Oh, no," Tory moaned softly.

Her mother smiled for the first time. "No, indeed. I persuaded Gerald, er, Mr. Emerson that is, to call on an old friend of his this morning. Lord Wilson is a very clever fellow. He will know what the best thing to do is, and I would be very much surprised if he agreed to our slipping out of town with our tails between our legs."

Tory was surprised into a little laugh. "Why, Mama, what a thing to say," she exclaimed. She had always thought her mother a silly woman with more hair than sense, but now she wondered how she could have been so misled. Just look how she had handled a difficult husband.

Her mother proved to be right, for when a chastened Gerald Emerson returned an hour later, they discovered that Lord Wilson had indeed put paid to any sudden flight. Instead they were to go about with heads held high, ignoring any sly comments or muffled laughter. And Mr. Emerson was to allow his daughter her former freedom as well, a situation that had taken Lord Wilson's utmost powers of persuasion.

"For heaven's sake, man," he had said in exasperation. "Can't you see why the ton laughs? It's as plain as the nose on your face! Here's your daughter, a woman of twenty-one who should by all rights be married already, and you hover over her as if she were a flighty fourteen you'd caught making up to one of the grooms! Take a good look at yourself, and see if I don't have the right of it. Your Victoria is a woman of sense; you've told me so often enough. Acknowledge that sense; open that cage you've been keeping her in!

"Furthermore, if you really want to silence the chatter and the ridicule, you'll let her see as many young sprigs of fashion as she cares to." He ignored his friend's moan, and continued, "And do what you can to get her into Rockford's company quickly."

"What?" Gerald Emerson had roared, half rising from his chair. "Never! I'll not have my precious Victoria anywhere near that gambling rake!"

"Then, you will be remarkably foolish, and not the astute man I have always thought you," Lord Wilson said coolly. "What else could quiet the gossip faster than for the ton to see that far from being over-possessive, indeed, obsessed with your daughter, you allow her to go about and see whomever she chooses. And when that includes Nicholas Sinclair, the Marquess of Rockford, what is there to mock?

"After all, little harm can come to her on a stroll with him in Hyde Park some afternoon at five. He's hardly about to drag her into the bushes and ravish her, if that's what you're afraid of. Not with all the crowds about. And if he takes her up in his curricle, he'll have his hands full of reins. You worry too much, Gerald. Besides, I've never heard Rockford accused of damaging a young lady of quality, and I don't believe he's about to start now. It's only his mistresses that have given him the name 'rake.' And who among us has not had an exciting armful in our keeping at one time or another in our lives, hmm?"

He poked his friend in the ribs and whispered, "Remember your redheaded Molly, Gerald? Hmm?"

Mr. Emerson had been forced to smile weakly, but it took several more minutes of impassioned argument before he was brought reluctantly to agree with his friend's proposals. But if he had not been such a proud man, with such a horror of being laughed at, he would never have agreed at all.

Now he said to his wife and stunned daughter, "Victoria is to be seen everywhere, with anyone she pleases. I do implore you, however, my dear, to exercise discretion."

"Do you mean you forbid me to speak to the Marquess of Rockford?" Tory asked, determined to get that straight.

Her father closed his eyes for a moment before he said, "No, I am not doing that. Lord Wilson said you must seek him out without delay, for when the ton sees you in his company, they will realize the dastardly mistake they have made. But I remind you, Victoria, it will only be necessary to be seen with him *briefly*. My objections to that blackguard remain unchanged, and if it weren't for the necessity of having to diffuse this gossip about us—well, I shall say no more. I am sure you will conduct yourself well, puss, now won't you?"

Tory assured him she would do so, and went off to pen a note to Bart Whitaker asking him to call and take her for a walk in the park later that afternoon.

Mr. Whitaker was agreeable, and at half past four, the two set out. Tory was glad her father had sequestered himself in the library, so Bart did not have to listen to a spate of instructions about her well-being, and the exact moment she was expected home.

She was extremely nervous, her stomach jumping in a peculiar way, and she did not care for it in the slightest. She had dressed very carefully in a new promenade gown of merino crepe, in shades of pale green that was trimmed with velvet and completed with a darker green bonnet and matching sandals.

"It's good to see you again, Tory," Bart said as they paused to let a hackney cab pass before crossing the street. "I've missed you."

"I've missed everything," Tory said dryly. "But thanks to our being ridiculed the other evening, my father has relented and I am to go about as before. You did hear of it, didn't you? I am sure it must be all over London by now."

He pressed her hand where it lay on his arm. "Yes, of course it is. But it will soon be a thing of the past when society sees you in company again. Er, without your father's hanging about you, that is."

Tory sighed. "I do love him, Bart, you know I do. But lately I seem to be seeing him with different eyes. It is not right the way he hems me in—hovers over me. No one else's father acts like that. And it is not as if I were a giddy young thing or even a hoyden always tying my garter in public, and you know it."

Bart grinned down at her. "No, no! You have always been a model of propriety."

She looked up at him, saw the laughter in his eyes, and smiled back. "Do not be bringing up any early sins now," she scolded. "They are as long gone as my childhood."

When they entered the park gates, Tory made

herself take a deep breath, hating herself for being so nervous. And not of society, either. Rather because she might very well come face-to-face with Nicholas Sinclair, and she was not at all sure what she would do if she did.

"Stop worrying," her escort said, nodding to some friends nearby. "In fact, relax. You look like someone being led to Newgate. Hardly flattering to me. Besides, no one will ask any rude questions. All you must do is pretend nothing untoward has happened at all."

"I know," Tory whispered, ignoring Mrs. Hawley, who was going by in an open landau with friends. The lady's mouth had dropped open, and she leaned forward so precariously, she was in danger of falling to the roadway. Tory told herself she was very bad to hope she did.

She and Whitaker stopped several times to chat with friends and acquaintances, and although Tory could see that everyone was dying to question her, good manners prevented it. For that she was exceedingly grateful. But she did not really relax until they were joined by her cousin Anne, just taking leave of a friend when they approached. The lady was easily persuaded to take Whitaker's other arm.

"I shall not ask you now what terrible thing you did to send your father into his most ferocious, protective mode, Tory," she said with a smile for their escort. "Not with this gentleman present, that is. But understand I shall require a most detailed explanation the first time we are alone."

"I intend to call on you as soon as possible, cuz. I do so want to speak to you."

Lady Garen assured her she would be delighted, then changed the subject. Only a few moments later, Tory saw the Marquess of Rockford approaching in a dashing phaeton behind a highbred pair of grays. He was alone except for the tiger who clung to the rear perch. As she came to a sudden decision, Tory's hand tightened on Whitaker's arm.

"Bart, please signal Rockford, if you would be so kind," she dared to say. "There is something I would ask him."

Obediently Whitaker raised his hand, and the marquess halted his pair beside them.

"Ladies, Whitaker," he said bowing over the reins. His voice was cold and controlled.

Tory sensed the tiger's eyes on her face, and in spite of the butterflies in her stomach, and her real horror of being considered fast, she made herself say, "I wonder if you would do me a kindness, m'lord?" Before he could reply, she hurried on, "I have been longing to drive behind your pair. Could I persuade you to take me up for a circuit of the park?"

Rockford's brows lifted, but he said smoothly, "Of course, ma'am. It would be my pleasure. Whitaker, if you would assist Miss Emerson? I shall return her shortly."

Once seated beside Sinclair, Tory was suddenly speechless. She was, however, very aware of him on the narrow seat, of his height and strength and masculinity.

To her surprise, the marquess halted again around the first bend. "Off you get, Toby," he said over his shoulder. "Wait for me here."

"Righto, guv," the boy said as he jumped off. Tory didn't dare look his way.

"Are you sure it is all right to do that?" she asked instead as the grays began to trot again. "I mean, there's been enough gossip about me as it is."

"There won't be anymore. In an open carriage it

is not necessary to have a servant playing goose-berry. And I thought you might prefer to speak to me without Toby hanging on your every word."

"Thank you," Tory breathed, looking down at where her hands were clasped tightly on her lap.

"I must say, however, this demure young thing I have beside me is a new come-out," he went on. "Can this truly be the witty, sometimes acerbic Victoria Emerson who is now so reticent, so shy?"

Tory bit back a retort. "I am finding it a little difficult to begin after the way we parted the last time we spoke," she admitted.

He thought for a moment. "At the Carleton party, you mean, when your father all but tore you from my side? Ah, yes. If I remember correctly, you had been chastising me for my bad habits, declaring you never wanted to see or talk to me again. And blaming me for Sperling's suicide as well.

"You can imagine my amazement when you asked me to take you up today. But perhaps that was only because you have thought of several other character faults of mine you wish to bring to my attention? Please do not spare me, Miss Emerson. We are alone now, and you have me at your mercy."

Thirteen

Tory remembered Sinclair's tiger had said he was heartsore, withdrawn, sad. He did not sound that way to her. He only sounded sarcastic, and she wondered if she had made a terrible mistake, making the first move as the boy had insisted she must.

"I have nothing more to say about your character, sir. That was not why I asked you to take me up," she said, still not looking at him.

"Force yourself to smile at me," he ordered before she could go on. "If you do not, people will wonder. And talk. It is not so hard, after all. Look at me!"

She turned, startled to see his gray eyes blazing down into hers. Then he smiled at her, a warm, intimate smile that curled her toes inside her sandals, before he transferred his attention to the team again. She smiled tentatively in return, but when she saw Mrs. Hawley's landau going by again, she leaned closer and gave him back his smile, with interest.

"Excellent," he said. She wondered if she were just imagining the constriction in his voice. "That should put paid to any lingering chat about your father's possessiveness. They've been calling you the lady behind the moat, you know. Your father is featured as the dragon at your gates."

He stopped speaking abruptly, his mouth clamped

shut. A white line formed around it. Glancing sideways, Tory shivered.

"What is it?" she asked. "Why do you look so angry?"

"I should have guessed," he said bitterly, after a moment to compose himself. "That is the reason you asked me to take you around the park, isn't it? To show the world *he* permits you to be alone with me? That there is no enmity between us? It never had anything to do with you *wanting* to see me, did it? Be with me because you missed me? Tell me, Miss Emerson, did he *order* you to do this? Is he even now waiting at home to learn of the successful conclusion? What a fool I've been!"

He laughed harshly, and the grays shied a little.

Tory cringed at that laugh, even as she wondered what she was to do now. But she could not bear to lie to him, so she said, "Yes, I will admit I thought it might be wise to be seen in your company. But it was not just that! I did want to see you, talk to you, truly, I did."

In her eagerness to make him understand, she put her hand on his arm. He stared at it for a moment, and she flushed and removed it.

"Even though you disapprove of me?" he demanded. "Even though you consider me no better than a murderer?"

"I—I, well, perhaps I judged you too quickly, sir. I have been told it was only your misfortune that Mr. Sperling came to grief over his debts to you. It could have been anyone. I shall never approve of gambling, but I do not know . . . I am so confused!"

He did not smile. "*You* are," he muttered instead. "Tell me, ma'am, where does all this leave us? We'll be coming around to where we left Whitaker and your cousin shortly. Shall I see you again, or may I expect another charming snub from your father?"

"I hope we will meet. As for my father, I do not know what he will do, but I suspect he might be agreeable to a dance every now and again, or perhaps a moment or two of conversation."

"This far but no further, eh? Good of him," Sinclair sneered.

"I am sorry. It is just the way he is."

"I'm well aware of the way he is. It's sickening. He has kept you his darling little girl, his own private pet, for too long. Have you ever thought that perhaps he intends to keep you his forever?"

Tory gasped a little. "No, that can't be! He may be a little overprotective where I am concerned . . ."

She ignored the marquess's snort of derision and rushed on, "I mean, of course he intends for me to marry someday. He speaks of it often."

"How?" came the blunt retort. "As something he hopes will happen soon? Or does he perhaps mention a time far in the future?"

Tory fell silent. She knew her father still felt she was not ready for marriage. She had never understood why. But could what the marquess was implying be true? Could her father be trying to keep her his, and no other man's? She shivered again, praying that was not the case.

"There is Whitaker and your cousin ahead," Sinclair said as he slowed the team. "Think about what I have said, Miss Emerson. It would be such a shame if such as you were kept behind that moat forever, guarded by the wicked dragon."

Speechless, Tory let Bart help her down. She had to summon all her wits to thank the marquess. She was glad her voice didn't shake as she did so.

Later, she found both her mother and father

waiting to question her about whom she had spoken to and seen. She told them that Rockford had taken her up for a turn and watched her mother's complacent nod while her father paled and looked distraught.

"What did he say? Was he rude to you? Forward? Did he make any suggestions for further meetings alone? Did he dare to *touch* you? Come now, I'll have an answer, miss!"

"He did none of those things, Papa," Tory said, her heart sinking at this additional evidence of her father's eccentricity. "He was a perfect gentleman."

"Ha!" her father said as he paced to and fro. "Well, now society has seen you with him, it will be unnecessary for you to do anything more but nod slightly if you chance to meet."

"I do not think that will serve, sir," Tory persisted, although she was quaking inwardly at her daring, and praying she did not arouse his anger.

To her relief, her mother spoke up. "Indeed, Mr. Emerson, one meeting is not like to silence the gossiping. What are you thinking of? And no harm will come to Victoria, you know, for she will see the marquess only in the company of others."

"He is the kind of man who lures girls out to dark terraces so he can have his way with them," Mr. Emerson insisted. "I tell you, I'll not have it! I'll not!"

Tory suddenly felt a great weariness, and she put her hand to her head. She did not think she could stand much more of this carping, this endless, endless preoccupation with her and any man who dared approach her.

"I do assure you, sir, the marquess has never offered me the slightest discourtesy. You do him a great disservice," she said with dignity.

Her father gaped at her for daring to contradict him, and his face turned purple with rage. "And I suppose he is not a great rake? A gambler who was responsible for his friend's death?" he asked sarcastically. "Leave me, Victoria! I am very displeased with you, to be so pert! To think you believe you know better than your elders the ways of the world. I tell you the man is no good! You will avoid him in the future."

It was extremely unfortunate that Lord Dorr should have chosen the following morning to make his declaration to Mr. Gerald Emerson, but he did not feel he could delay longer. He had seen Miss Emerson in Rockford's phaeton the previous day, and feared the girl might be growing fond of the marquess, and he of her. Accordingly he was on the doorstep in South Audley Street at ten, bearing a large bouquet of flowers for Mrs. Emerson and presenting his card to the Emerson butler.

The man he was desirous of seeing was not feeling at all well that morning. It was not just his daughter's unaccustomed defiance, although that certainly played a part in his ill humor. But his rheumatism was acting up, and his knee was so painful this morning, he could hardly bear to stand on it.

He was tempted to deny the young man, but he had a very good idea why he had called, and he wished to send him about his business without further ado. As Lord Dorr came in and bowed, he eyed the flowers the young man was clutching with a jaundiced eye, not even tempted to chuckle at the ridiculous picture he presented.

"Yes?" he said.

It was not the most gracious beginning, but Lord

Dorr was not to be deterred. He had practiced his speech several times before his mirror so he would not stammer or hesitate, and now, he launched into that speech.

Gerald Emerson stared at him as he charged ahead, telling of his great love for Miss Emerson, his fervent desire to make her his wife, and concluding with his financial situation.

"I do assure you, dear sir, I am as able to care for Miss Emerson as you would yourself. And when my father dies, I shall be the Earl of Gramere, and your daughter, a countess."

He lowered his eyes from the ceiling then for the first time, and when he saw Gerald Emerson's ferocious frown, he hastened to add, "Not that I am looking forward to my father's demise! Of—of course not, sir! I only mentioned it because some people feel such things are important, titles, y'know, well, my mother thinks so anyway, but I'm sure you would not, that is, I mean where your beloved daughter is concerned, what is a title, after all . . ." he gasped, finally ending his sentence.

"No," Gerald Emerson said in the welcome silence.

"No?" Lord Dorr echoed. "But—but, sir, why do you object?"

"I've no objection to you at all. I simply do not care to have my daughter marry at this time. She is too young."

"Er, but, sir, I believe Miss Emerson is twenty-one? My—my sister married at seventeen . . ."

"Is she happy?" Emerson interrupted, leaning forward over his desk.

Lord Dorr looked confused. His sister's happiness—or lack of it—had never concerned him. He frowned a little as he said, "Well, of course she must be, don't you think? They've had the heir already, less than a year after the wedding. I don't generally care for babies, but I must say he's a cute little nipper, so you see . . ."

He fell silent again as Gerald Emerson stated, "I tell you my daughter shall not wed now. I have nothing more to say to you, sir. Good day."

"But may I hope that sometime in the future she will be allowed to marry?" the young peer persisted. "I would wait forever!"

Gerald Emerson stared at the eager suitor, noting his flushed face, the wilted condition of a cravat he suspected had taken an age for Dorr to perfect, and the sorry-looking bunch of flowers he had mangled in his eagerness, and he felt a surprising rush of pity.

"We shall see," he said more moderately. "Early days, yet, you know. Be patient. We shall see."

Later Gerald Emerson informed his wife and daughter of the offer he had received for her hand. "Of course, I told the young idiot, no," he said as he accepted the cup of tea his wife had poured for him. "I assume that in this matter you do not question my judgment, Victoria?"

"Certainly not, sir," she said steadily. "I shall never want to marry Lord Dorr."

Her father beamed at her. "Yes, it is just as I told him. You are too young to fix your interest.

"I do warn you, however, to be on your guard this evening at the party you attend. How unfortunate this knee keeps me from going with you!

"Mary, keep your wits about you, now! You will be Victoria's sole chaperon and it is very important . . ."

Tory ceased to listen. She was reviewing her gowns, wondering which one she should wear, and wondering as well if Rockford would be there, and what she would do or say if he approached her. But when she stepped inside the crowded drawing room later as her mother paused to speak to some friends, the first person she encountered was Lady Clarissa Carr.

"Dear child, how glad I am to see you," that woman exclaimed. "Come with me. I have something I must say to you."

Mystified, Tory followed her away from the party down a long hall to a small room at the back of the house.

"There, just as I suspected, it's empty," Lady Carr said as she waved Tory to a chair opposite the one she had chosen. The room was lit only by a few candles, and delicately scented by a bowl of roses set on the center table.

"Miss Emerson, it has come to my attention that you and my dear friend Nicky Sinclair have been seeing a lot of each other. I would ask you your feelings for the marquess."

Tory stared at the white-haired little lady, more than a little appalled.

As if she knew how outrageous her question had been, Clarissa Carr laughed merrily. "I know," she said. "I have never had an ounce of tact. But you see, my dear, I was one of Nicky's mother's best friends. And when she died, I made a vow that I would take her place with him, as far as I was able. I don't think he has been a happy man for quite a while. Do you know why?"

Tory found she could not look away from that concerned, kindly old face. "No, not really. It is true we see each other on occasion, but we are not as close as you seem to think, ma'am. That is, there is no romantic attachment between us."

"No? How unfortunate! I was thinking at my garden fete—and the Duchess of Norwood quite agreed with me—that marrying you would be the making of Nicky. He does so need an anchor."

Telling herself she would not let that unfortunate simile weigh with her, Tory nodded a little. It was all she could think of to do.

"I mean that he has been adrift ever since his family all died. He has no one to care for, and he lets no one care for him. I had such *great* hopes that you and he might have—well, no matter."

She rose then and smoothed her skirts. "Would you excuse me me for a moment, my dear? I must visit the ladies' withdrawing room, but I do have more to say. Would I be imposing on you if I asked you to wait for my return?"

Tory had risen as well, and she shook her head. Promising to be back shortly, Lady Carr hurried from the room.

Tory wondered what she was letting herself in for. She could not imagine what else the unpredictable lady might have to say, but she was intrigued enough to remain, even though she wondered what her mother would think if she knew.

She was admiring the bowl of roses when she heard a slight noise behind her, and she turned with a smile. But instead of Clarissa Carr, Nicholas Sinclair stood in the doorway. As her hand crept to her throat, he came in and closed the door behind him.

"Lady Carr said she was sure I would like the surprise she had arranged for me here. I do, indeed," he said as he came to stand close before Tory.

"It was done without my knowledge, sir, I can assure you of that," Tory said, angry now at the way she had been tricked. "Stand aside! I intend to leave this room immediately."

"Oh, come, where's the harm? And you said yourself there was small chance of our being allowed to converse from now on. Why shouldn't we take advantage of Lady Carr's kindness? I see your father did not come tonight. He'll never know of it."

"No, he has had a reoccurrence of his rheumatism and was unable. But I must leave you, sir. My mother is here, and she will be wondering where I am. . . ."

"No, she won't," he told her, still standing much too close for Tory's peace of mind. "She's been captured and carried off by Lady Carr for a private coz, and is too much in alt at this great honor to even notice you are missing.

"Victoria?" he asked in a softer voice. "Won't you stay with me? For just a little while?"

He stared down into her face, his deep-set gray eyes intent. "Forgive me, but you seem a little troubled this evening. What is it?" he asked, as if he knew she could not answer him. Or wouldn't.

"I do? How can you tell? No one else has remarked on it."

Still, his eyes searched her face. "Perhaps no one else looks at you as closely as I do," he said.

"It is a private family matter. I cannot speak of it," she said at last, moving away from him to the other side of the table. The scent of the roses was heady between them.

"Your father, no doubt. Has he been at you again, my dear?

"I heard in White's this afternoon that Lord Dorr was wearing a long face. Can it be he called on your father and put his puppylike devotion to the test?"

"It is not kind of you to mock the viscount," Tory reproved him. "He is a nice young man, and he means well."

"By which I gather he not only did not attain your father's blessing, his failure to do so did not bother you a bit. I am relieved."

"You are not relieved at all," Tory lashed out, stung into hasty speech. "You know very well I don't care a snap of my fingers for Lord Dorr! It is all some sort of game with you. . . ."

He moved so swiftly around the table, she was startled. Taking her in his arms, he stared down at her for a moment before he bent and kissed her. Once again, Tory closed her eyes and gave herself up to the myriad sensations his kiss invoked. This time her hands did creep up around his neck, and as they buried themselves in his dark hair, his own arms tightened around her. His mouth moved on hers, at first softly, then with a growing intensity she was powerless to withstand, even if she had wanted to. There was faint music coming from the drawing room where a string quartet played, and the roses still perfumed the air, but Tory was aware of nothing but his lips covering hers, the feel of his hard body against her, chest and hips and thighs— the dizzying way his hands caressed her back. When he released her, she did not open her eyes. Instead she tried to memorize their embrace so she would never forget it.

"No, it is not, Victoria," he said, his voice wondering, and more than a little unsteady. "It is not a game."

Her eyes flew open, and she stared at him. "No?" she whispered.

He shook his head, his hands lingering on the

bare skin between the puffed sleeves of her gown and the top of the long evening gloves she wore.

"I love you," he said quietly. "I never thought I would ever say those words, but I find to my infinite amazement, and most humble chagrin, that if I do not, I shall never be happy again. I want you, Victoria, I want you for my love, my bride, my wife. I want to live with you as long as we both have breath. I want to share your life—all your joys and sorrows. I want to be your husband. Know I will always cherish you, always adore you, always keep you safe."

Tory listened, hardly breathing. Was it possible she was really hearing Rockford correctly? she wondered. Was he, of all people, claiming he loved her?

She brushed a hand over her eyes, as if to clear them. He picked up that hand and put it to his chest under his dark evening coat.

"Can you feel my heart?" he asked quietly. "From this moment, it beats only for you."

"Oh, Nicholas," she cried, her eyes filling with tears, "What a beautiful thing to say!"

"I think love has made me a poet," he told her with a rueful grin. Then his face grew serious again, and he continued, "But I must know how you feel about me. Do you think you could ever learn to love me someday?"

Tory swallowed. She knew what she intended to say was brazen, but she did not care. "Someday?" she echoed, lifting her head to look up into his eyes. "But I love you now, my dear. I think I have since the day we pretended together at the garden fete."

She was allowed to say no more, for his eager kisses covered her face, and he murmured his love again into her dark hair.

Eventually when a little reason returned, they

sat down together on a sofa and, holding hands, began to make plans.

"I shall call on your father tomorrow," he told her.

Tory was jolted back to earth from the cloud she had been occupying this past half hour. "Oh, no, you must not!" she cried. "He will only say no, if he doesn't shoot you for daring to aspire to my hand. I've told you what he is like!"

"I know. I also know a formal application will be to no avail. But you do see, as an honorable man, I must try."

"He'll keep me from you," Tory warned. "He'll take me back to the country, and I'll never see you again."

"You believe so? You honestly think I would not come to you no matter where he hid you? But I shan't let him take you anywhere."

He bent his head over hers to kiss her, but Tory held him away. "Please, Nicholas," she said, her eyes pleading, "can't we wait just a bit? I mean, before you call on my father? This has all happened so fast, I am confused, dizzy almost."

"Perhaps I had something to do with that?" he asked in a husky voice.

"Of course you did. But do say you agree to wait for a few days at least. I would talk to my cousin Anne, get her advice. She is very wise, and very kind."

For a moment Tory thought he would refuse, but at last he nodded. "But only till the end of the week, love," he said. "Stand up, now."

Mystified, Tory did as she was bid, to find him taking her in charge like some fussy lady's maid. As he straightened her skirts, puffed her sleeves and tucked a wayward curl into place, he said, "Best you get back to the party. We have been here too long. I'll take my leave. There'll be no trouble for only Lady Carr saw me arrive.

"I can do nothing about your mouth," he added, his gaze caressing it. "Hopefully your mother will not notice."

"What's wrong with it?" she asked, going to the mirror over the mantelpiece to study it. Yes, it was a little swollen, but personally she thought her eyes might give her away faster. They looked like two stars, and she did not seem to be able to stop smiling.

"Put some cold water on your lips before you rejoin the company," Sinclair said, coming up behind her to kiss the back of her neck. "And now, before I completely undo all this perfection I have just achieved, I'd better go."

He paused at the door, looked back at her, and said quietly just before he opened it, "Take care, my love. You are very dear to me."

Fourteen

JUST AS THE marquess had predicted, Tory had no trouble with her mother that evening, for her long absence from the drawing room had not even been noticed. Indeed, Mrs. Emerson could do nothing on the way home but enthuse about Lady Clarissa Carr and the long, intimate talk they had shared. Lady Carr had even invited her to visit her home near Richmond so she might have a private tour of the famous gardens, and Mary Emerson was already wondering which ensemble she should wear for such an august occasion. Tory nodded and smiled, but in reality she was not even in the Emerson coach being driven home from yet another evening party. No, instead she was in Nicholas Sinclair's arms, reliving his passionate kisses.

She overslept the following morning, but when she finally opened her eyes, he was the first person she thought of, and for a moment she could only snuggle down under the covers and smile at her great good fortune. He loved her! He truly loved her! She must remember to thank God for him and the marvelous future they were soon to share.

Thinking of that jolted her from her reveries, and as her father's angry face replaced the marquess's in her mind, she rose and scurried to the dressing room. As she rang the bell for her maid, she frowned. She must hurry to Anne as soon as she was dressed. Perhaps her cousin would have some suggestions about what she and Nicholas should do.

As usual, she found Anne seated at her desk in her sunny drawing room. Tory had wondered in the past what kept Anne so busy there, so often, but she had never inquired, nor did she think to do so now in her preoccupation.

Lady Garen noticed her pent-up urgency, and was quick to tell her butler that she was on no account to be disturbed by anyone, before she came and drew Tory down on a sofa beside her.

"Tell me," she ordered.

A torrent of words washed over her as Tory told her of Nicholas Sinclair and the love they shared.

"He wanted to speak to my father today, but I persuaded him to wait till the end of the week," Tory concluded. "Oh, Anne, I know my father will be furious! Of course, there is no hope he will say yes. And no pleading of mine is apt to change his mind."

"No, of course it won't," her cousin agreed.

"Yesterday Papa refused Lord Dorr, claiming once again I was not ready for marriage. If I remember correctly, he said I was too young to have fixed my interest. Well, now I have done just that, but he will refuse to see it that way. He hates Nicholas so!"

"Because of his character?"

Tory shook her head. "I don't think it is just that, although that is what he claims. No, I think it is because somehow he suspects I am attracted to him."

Lady Garen did not speak for a moment, then she

said, "Tell me, my dear, and do not fly up into the boughs, now!—are you *sure* of this love you have for the marquess? I mean, your father's dislike of Rockford has some solid reason behind it, even taking into account his obsession with you. The man is an inveterate gambler, a rake as well. I do not know how many women he has had in his keeping, but it is said their number is astounding."

"He has changed," Tory said, her eyes stormy. "There is no mistress now. And he has not gambled this age."

"But when his luck sours and he can find partners again, won't he begin anew?"

"No, he won't," Tory exclaimed. "I'll see to it he doesn't!"

Anne rose to adjust a drapery so the sun would not shine in their faces. "I know you believe you can change him, but my dear, I must tell you when people are addicted, such a thing is impossible. They are the only ones who can stop. Neither you nor anyone else on this earth can do it for them. Trust me. I know this."

She sighed and rubbed her forehead for a moment as she took her seat again. "My late husband's father could not stop drinking," she said, her voice steady. "No matter how his wife—all his family—pleaded with him, no matter how ill he became, he continued. And trying to keep drink from him only made him cunning. He had bottles hidden everywhere. At last, of course, he drank himself to death. He was only forty-five."

"Nicholas is not like that," Tory said, her face ashen.

"Is gambling any better than drinking? It is only another addiction. You must face facts, not hide from them. It is entirely possible that in a year or

164

so, Rockford will run through his fortune, perhaps yours as well, if your father can be persuaded to release it to you. You may end up hungry, in want, with a weakling who promises he will never touch a deck of cards again, who then takes the housekeeping money and does just that. Think well, my dear. It is all your life, marriage."

Tory looked down at her hands in their neat tan kid gloves. She swallowed hard, afraid the tears she could feel coming would appear and disgrace her. But why was Anne being so difficult? She had come to her for help, not criticism. And here she was, pointing out all these horrid things. She didn't know Nicholas, she couldn't know him, to malign him so. But *she* did, and she loved him. If there were troubles ahead, she could handle them, she knew, for deep in her heart she believed in him.

She looked up into Anne's concerned face and made herself smile. "I do not think I have to worry about his gambling any more, cuz, truly I don't. Do not ask me how I know that, however. It is just a deep, calm conviction I have. As for his mistresses, well, if he sets one up again, I shall only have myself to blame, now won't I?"

Her cousin shook her head, but she smiled a little, too.

"Very well, Tory. I have done all I could to bring you to your senses, but it is obvious to me I could talk to you from now to next year, and I wouldn't be able to change your mind. Ah, love! How powerful it is.

"Now, let us discuss what you are to do when your father refuses the marquess, as he is sure to do. We must pray he does not run him through as well, of course."

"As if Nicholas would let him," Tory scoffed, feeling happier now she knew Anne was on their side. "I have been thinking of that," she went on seriously now. "Of course the first thing Papa will do is whisk me down to the country. Nicholas says he won't let that happen, but I do not see how it can be avoided. And I am afraid that, once out of town, it will be impossible for me to escape."

"What can you do, then?"

"There is only one thing we can do. Run away together before Papa takes me back to Devon."

"You would consider Scotland?"

Tory did not look away from her cousin's cool, considering gaze. Everything she had been taught all her life made her cringe away from the desperate, often fatal consequences of a marriage over the anvil, but for Nicholas Sinclair, she would do it if she had to.

"Yes, I would go to Gretna with him, and gladly," she said, her voice steady.

"I was only testing you, my dear. There is no need for such desperate measures," Anne said. "Have you forgotten you are of age now? All of one and twenty? You can marry whomever you please, and whenever you like."

"Why, to be sure, I can," Tory exclaimed, smiling broadly. "However did I come to forget that? And how grateful I am now that I am such an elderly debutante."

"I suggest you tell the marquess he must get a special license as soon as possible," Anne went on, bringing Tory back to earth again. "There is no telling what your father will do when he discovers you have left him for another man. I am afraid he might be dangerous. But once you are safely wed, there will be nothing he can do.

"If you like, you can write your Nicholas a note

now. I'll arrange for Bart to deliver it to him. In fact, why don't you suggest the two of you meet here? There are plans you must make together. Rockford can come here with Bart, supposedly to call, when you are here, and we can leave you alone together."

Tory threw her arms around her cousin and hugged her close. "Oh, Anne, thank you, thank you," she murmured. "You are so good to me! And I don't know what I would have done without you, truly, I don't."

Anne hugged her in return before she drew away. "Goose! I suspect you would have managed. But come. Don't you have a letter to write? A very important letter?"

As Tory began to get up, she added, "You know, I used to think your father's concern for you stemmed from his deep love. I even envied you that love. Now, however, I do not. I do not think his behavior is normal where you are concerned, not after the way he kept you prisoner. And for what? For talking to a peer of the realm who is invited everywhere, no matter his faults? Your father, Tory, is obsessed, and such men can be dangerous. Be very careful. Do not anger him this week if you can possibly avoid it."

Tory returned to Anne's house twice more that week. Each time she went, she had her usual spirited argument with her old governess about the advisability of her call, and the wisdom of going with only a footman or a maid in attendance.

Tory tried to behave normally, but the second time she left the house on South Audley Street, her impatience to be gone was obvious. Miss Essex thought for a while and then went down to knock on the library door.

Her story was soon told, for it was comprised only of conjecture and suspicions, and some carefully concealed jealousy that Tory could want any other companion than herself.

"Thank you for telling me this, Miss Essex," Emerson said, rising to terminate the interview when she began to repeat herself.

Miss Essex rose as well, a timid smile on her face for her employer.

"I do hope you will not think me fanciful, sir," she ventured to say. "I know how worried you have been about Victoria. And she has been so different since we came to town. Especially this week. There's something afoot. I know it."

She shook her head in dismay as Gerald Emerson ushered her to the door, trying not to hurry her along too obviously.

"No, you have done just what you ought, and I am grateful to you for your care of her," he said as he opened the door for her. Forgetting her in a moment, he ordered his butler to run and fetch him a hackney, and to step smartly for he was in a great hurry.

As he waited for the cab, Gerald Emerson paced his library impatiently. He had been feeling uneasy himself this week, although he could not put a name to his worries. But there had been something about Victoria suddenly, a blooming that made her so beautiful it was almost unearthly. And she smiled so often, hummed little snatches of tunes to herself as she ran up and down the stairs. He could not remember her doing that for a very long time. Had this anything to do with her calls on her cousin? Well, he would find out, he told himself grimly as he jammed his top hat on his head and picked up his gloves and cane when he heard the cab in the street beyond his window.

Lady Garen lived on Arlington Street near Green Park. It was a quiet neighborhood, and when he saw not one, but two carriages drawn up before her door, Emerson realized Miss Essex may well have hit on something significant. He recognized his own carriage at a glance. He did not know the smart phaeton beyond it. A *gentleman's* phaeton, he told himself harshly as he ordered the hackney driver to pull up across the street where he would have a good view of Lady Garen's front door. And as far as he knew, Anne Garen did not receive gentlemen callers. She never had, being the most unnatural woman he had ever known. After her husband's early death, he had fully expected her to marry again, and had even called on her to offer his services finding her another groom. She had only laughed at him, and sent him away. He had resented that, of course, and had never really forgiven her.

Inside the house, Lady Garen had left her cousin and the marquess to the solitude of the drawing room, while she and Bart Whitaker had adjourned to the library. The lovers barely waited for the doors to close behind them before they were in each other's arms. It was a long time before either spoke.

"You had best sit over there, love," Nicholas said at last, pointing to a distant chair. "You bewitch me so, I forget we have plans to make."

Tory smiled at him as she drew him down on the sofa beside her. "I shall behave myself, never fear, sir," she said.

"But can I?" he asked no one in particular.

Tory laughed in delight, and he bent to kiss her throat, his fingers soft on her face.

"Come now, sir, let us begin," she said a little unsteadily. "You are still determined to speak to my father in two days' time?"

"I must," he told her, sitting back. "It is the only honorable thing I can do."

"And I tell you he will have me from London by dawn the following day," Tory said gloomily, as she had before. "You say you can stop him, but how do you propose to do that? He is my father, and until we are married, he can take me wherever he likes. There is nothing you can do."

He reached out and took her hands in his to squeeze them. "Victoria, listen to me," he said so earnest that her eyes widened. "I tell you he cannot keep you from me. And if it were only a matter of waiting for you until he relented, I would wait for as long as that took. But we both know he won't relent. So here is what I think we should do. I propose to call on him at eleven in the morning. Could you be sure you are not at home then? Perhaps you could seek sanctuary with your cousin. Then, when I have his answer, I will come here to you directly. We will leave London immediately for Tye, my estate on the southern coast. I am afraid there has been a slight delay with the special license—the bishop has been ill—but I expect to have it to hand then.

"Your father may well come and badger Lady Garen, but I think her more than capable of handling him."

"But how wonderful you are to have thought of such a marvelous plan, Nicholas," Tory exclaimed. "Of course that is what we must do."

She looked away from him for a moment, then

said a little diffidently, "You know, Anne tried to talk me out of this marriage. She said you were addicted to gambling and would ruin the both of us before you were through. That I would end unhappy, perhaps in want."

In the short silence that followed her speech, Tory did not dare look Sinclair's way.

"Did she now?" he said at last. "I have not gambled for a long time, Victoria. I feel no urge to begin again, none at all. Yet I cannot *promise* I won't, for I simply do not know. I am asking you to take a terrible gamble yourself, love, for I am asking you to wager on *me*. Believe me when I say I will do everything I can to make you happy, and if it is at all humanly possible, you will never be in want."

Tory put her arms around him and drew him close. "That is all I wanted to hear, dearest," she said, her voice breaking. "I will gladly gamble on you—anytime."

When the knock on the door came a few minutes later, the two lovers drew apart reluctantly. Lady Garen had decreed meetings alone of only half an hour, and she was an excellent timekeeper. Of course, to Tory and Sinclair, it seemed more a matter of a few minutes, but they were so grateful to her, they said nothing.

And besides, Tory reminded herself, in a little while they would be together forever.

The four talked a bit about the coming interview with Gerald Emerson, for Bart Whitaker was a full conspirator now. Anne applauded Sinclair's plan to leave London immediately after the interview, and assured him she was more than a match for the man, bluster and rage at her though he would.

"I shall of course be here, m'lady, to assist you," Bart told her, and the determination on his long

171

face told her there was no way she could refuse his offer.

"Perhaps it would be better if you left London for a while as well, cuz," Tory said, worried now for her cousin's safety, Mr. Whitaker or no. "You could visit friends in the country, couldn't you?"

"No, no, there is no need for that," Anne Garen protested. "My uncle will have no proof you left from here, for I shall simply maintain that although, yes, you did call that morning, it was for a brief time only. We will have to do something about your maid, your father's coachman, and the carriage, however."

"Why don't I simply dismiss them, as I so often do?" Tory asked. "I shall say you will be bringing me home in your carriage. You can tell Papa you rather thought I took a hackney to the dressmakers where I was to meet Mama."

Whitaker looked at Nick Sinclair and grinned. "Did you ever hear such a pair, Rockford?" he asked. "Scheming away like two old hands, not gently reared ladies of quality. I shall never understand women, never."

"Just as well for you, my good man," Anne Garen said, and they all laughed.

A few minutes later, the three rose to take their leave, Tory tying the ribbons of the bonnet she had discarded earlier.

It was a lovely day, and they lingered for a moment on the pavement before Anne's house, exchanging good-byes.

Across the street, Gerald Emerson clutched the side of the hackney cab with a hand that had gone white at the knuckles. Was it possible, he asked himself, horrified. Was it possible his darling Victoria had been closeted in her cousin's house with that blackguard, Rockford?

He watched her closely, and he saw the smile she gave the man, the way her hand lingered in his, and he stiffened. Victoria had never smiled at *him* that way! Then she turned toward him, and her expression almost undid him. It was obvious she was in love with the fellow, why, it was plain as plain could be. And he, yes, he was smiling, too, lifting her hand to his lips to kiss, and holding it until Bartholomew Whitaker called him to order and he was forced to assist her into her carriage. But of course he would smile, when such a beautiful, seductive plum had fallen right into his open hand, Emerson told himself, gritting his teeth in his agony.

As his daughter's carriage drove away, he continued to glare at the Marquess of Rockford. With all his heart he wished he had thought to bring his pistols with him, for if he had, Rockford would be lying in the gutter now, bleeding to death for daring—yes, *daring* to corrupt her! And he, no matter what the consequences he had to face, would be glad.

Fifteen

As soon as Bart Whitaker had been dropped off at his rooms on Upper Brook Street, Toby spoke up from his perch at the rear of the phaeton.

"Got trouble, guv," he said. "Lots of trouble."

Nick Sinclair, his mind intent on the call he intended to make on his man of business, barely listened. He had to tell Abner Barrett of his approaching nuptials, and arrange for money to be forwarded to him for their stay at Tye. Just thinking of Victoria there in his house, his bed, made his eyes light up, and his mouth curve in a contented smile. Soon, he told himself. Very soon now. And then there was the special license to fetch, the most beautiful wedding ring he could find to buy, and . . .

"I said there's trouble ahead, guv," Toby persisted.

"Hmm? What kind of trouble?" Nick asked as he headed for the city.

"While you were in Lady Garen's house with Miss Emerson, there was a man watching the house. He was in a hackney cab across the street."

"I didn't notice," Nick said absently.

Toby snorted. "You wouldn't notice an elephant what got loose from the Royal Enclosure if you was with Miss Emerson," he retorted.

"True," his master said, grinning openly now.

"I tell you, I didn't like the look of him, guv," Toby went on. "He was an older gent with a red face, and he looked mean."

Nick thought for a moment and then he shrugged. There was no way Tory's father could have found out about their trysts, not in such a short time. No doubt Toby was seeing ogres where there were none. "It's a public thoroughfare. Anyone can use it," he said in dismissal.

"Yes, but . . ."

"Enough," Nick ordered. "Be quiet, if you know what's good for you! I've a lot on my mind."

Toby subsided, but he looked stormy and every once in a while his lips moved slightly as he scolded his master under his breath.

Several streets away, Tory had arrived home, and she went immediately to her room. She needed a few minutes alone to compose herself, as she always did after a meeting with Nicholas. Time to review his words, his kisses, and time then to put them away so no one in the household would notice anything unusual about her. Nicholas made her feel such incandescent joy, she was sure she must glow with it like a rocket in the dark night sky.

Then, too, Essie rarely intruded in her bedroom, and she knew her mother was out. She imagined her father busy with his papers in the library as was his custom this time of day.

But only a short time later, as she was drying her hands in the dressing room, she heard his raised voice as he came up the stairs. For a moment her heart jumped in alarm, and she had to take a deep breath to calm herself.

He did not knock, but merely threw open the door. Tory winced as it crashed against the wall.

"Where are you?" he demanded. "Come here at once!"

Tory made herself enter the bedroom again, and she gasped when she saw his face, so furious it was purple.

"Jezebel!" he roared, shaking his fist at her.

Tory stood frozen beside her bed. He knew! Somehow or other he had found out about Nicholas— their love for each other. She felt her heart sink, for now he would keep them apart, and all their plans to be wed would be for naught.

"So, you thought to pull the wool over my eyes finely, did you, miss?" her father went on, striding up to where she stood. It took all her courage to face him, when she wanted so desperately to run to the dressing room and lock the door. Only knowing how futile such a move would be kept her in her place.

"I saw you today, brazen bawd that you are!" he bellowed. "Smirking at him, letting him kiss your hand—bah!"

A fine spray of his spittle hit her face, but Tory did not flinch.

"Well, you shall discover what happens to willful misses who think they know better than their fathers! Ones who disobey direct orders, cheat and lie! Yes, you shall not go unpunished for this, you bad, bad girl!"

He raised his hand then and slapped her. Unprepared for such a thing from a man who had never done such a thing in his life, Tory staggered and fell heavily onto the bed.

"Mr. Emerson! What on earth are you doing?" her mother's voice demanded from the doorway.

Tory put both hands over her face and tried to

176

control her sobs. The whole side of her face burned from the force of his blow.

"I'm punishing this vile daughter of ours, madam," he said. Between her fingers, Tory saw him raise his hand again, and she shuddered.

"No, my dear, you must not," Mary Emerson said, coming to grasp his arm to keep him from striking Tory again. "Whatever she has done, you must not beat her! Have you forgotten how you love her?"

"You do not know what she has done, Mary," he protested.

"No, but I suggest you come downstairs now and tell me about it. A nice cup of tea is what we need, and perhaps a little brandy to calm you. Come along, do."

As she spoke, she led him to the door. Not once had she looked at Tory or acknowledged her in any way.

"She must be locked in, then," Emerson said. "She must be guarded lest she escape and go to him. Yes, you stare, Mary. But she has been meeting that blackg . . ."

"Shh," his wife said firmly. "No more, now. Remember the servants, I beg. But lock the door, if it will make you feel better. She will be safe."

Tory heard the door close behind them, the key turn in the lock. Still, she did not move until the sound of their footsteps going down the stairs had died away.

She cried for a while then. Of course she cried for the pain she was feeling, but more for the death of her love for her father. There was no way she would ever feel the same about him after today.

It was growing dark when she finally rose and went to the dressing room to wash her tearstained face. Her eyes stared back at her from the mirror.

They looked empty, shuttered, as if they had never known any happiness. Her face was red from his blow, and she bathed it until the ache began to go away. It was then she realized how lucky she had been that her mother had come in when she did. Left to his own devices, who knew what Gerald Emerson might not have done to her.

Back in her room again, Tory lit some candles and settled down, her prayer book in her hand. She did not intend to read it, she held it merely for comfort. And when it fell open to the page where she had pressed the rosebud Nicholas had given her, she almost started to cry again.

No, there was no time for such weakness, she told herself firmly. Somehow or other she had to get away before her father took her from London and far from the Marquess of Rockford. He might not even take her home to Devon, she thought, panic rising in her breast. No, for he would know Nicholas could track her down there. Instead he might find some other place to keep her, and that would never do.

There was no one to help her. Essie was impossible. She fawned on her employer, thought his every word a pronouncement of great wisdom. She would never go against his will, not even for her former charge. And Nicholas would not know what had happened, for they had not planned to meet until after he had seen her father. As for Anne, the same held true.

For a moment, a great wave of despair washed over her, and she wanted to howl in frustration. Then she made herself go to the window. Her room was on the third floor. The tree outside was not tall enough to reach, and there was no handy, sturdy vine she might have climbed down. But looking down what seemed such a great distance to the ground, she doubted she would have had the courage to do that anyway. Besides, the garden was completely enclosed. Even if she could reach it safely, there was no escape from it except through the house. Certainly she could not hope to scale those ten-foot walls!

She would have to wait until she was released from this room. There was nothing else she could do. She sat for what seemed like hours, until at last her father unlocked the door. Two maids came in, one carrying her portmanteaus, the other with a tray of food. They were followed by a footman with her trunk.

After the footman left, the maids went to the dressing room to begin packing her clothes. And all the time, her father stood in the doorway, guarding it and glaring at her. He did not speak, perhaps because of the presence of the servants, and Tory was glad of that. She made no move to eat. Her stomach felt tied in knots, and under his ruthless surveillance, any appetite she might have had disappeared.

The maids finally finished after what seemed an endless time, and Gerald Emerson ushered them out before he slammed the door and locked it again.

It was dark now, although Tory had no idea of the hour. Beyond her door, the house hummed with activity as more trunks were brought down from the box room, and servants clattered up and down the stairs. Wearily she stretched out on her bed, and tried to doze.

It must have been very late when she woke. The house was quiet now, and it was easy to hear the key as it turned cautiously in the lock. She sat up, her heart pounding. Had her father returned to finish his punishment? she wondered, feeling panic surface again. But the large, comfortably padded figure who stood there, a finger to her lips, was her mother. She was dressed in her nightrobe and dressing gown, and she carried a candle that she set down on the center table after she had shut the door softly behind her.

"Mama," Tory breathed. "Why are you here?"

Her mother did not reply until she was close beside the bed. "Speak softly, Victoria," she cautioned. "Mr. Emerson is asleep now, but it would be ruinous if he were to hear us and come and investigate."

Tory felt a little stab of hope, but she only nodded.

"I've come to release you, Victoria," her mother went on, holding up the key to the room. "This is a duplicate that Cook had. You'll have to go tonight, soon. We are to take coach first thing tomorrow."

"But—but if you let me go, won't Papa be angry with you when he finds out? I wouldn't want him to hurt you!"

Her mother smiled a little. "He will never know. I've bribed one of the maids to run off tonight, too. He'll think she was the one who let you go."

"Why are you doing this?" Tory asked, for she had never known her mother to defy her husband, indeed, even disagree with him in any way. "He must have told you about my meeting with Nicholas Sinclair. And you must be angry with me, too."

"No, I'm not angry. You were bound to fall in love with someone sooner or later. I could wish you had chosen a better man, but there is nothing I can do about that.

"As for why I'm doing it, well, perhaps it will be better after you're gone. I always resented you, you know. No, of course you didn't know, for I pretended to love you as much as your father did. I never realized the extent of that resentment myself, until a little while ago.

"But from the moment you were born, my husband started to ignore me. *You* had all his love. He didn't even mind that we could have no more children."

She sighed, and continued, "It might have been easier all around if we had. If he had had four or five others to love, surely it would have diffused the intensity of his love for you."

Tory stared at her mother, barely breathing, as she went on, "You were such a beautiful baby, Victoria! He carried you everywhere with him, doted on you. And the first time you toddled across the room to him, arms stretched wide, and called him Da-da, he was hopelessly lost. You know how he has watched over you, spoiled you, fussed about you. Why, a little cold had him calling in the best doctors available! And when you got the chicken pox, I thought he would go out of his mind with worry that you would be scarred by it. He stayed up with you until he dropped to prevent that, then ordered the nurses to do so as well."

Her voice died away, and Tory took her hand. She had known of this, of course, but she had never suspected her mother's feelings. It was too bad it had had to be that way.

"I am grateful for your help, Mama," she said softly. "I hope all will be well with you now."

"After some time passes, perhaps we will be able to see each other again," Mary Emerson said, squeezing her daughter's hand to show she bore her no ill feeling. "And when you have children, perhaps Mr. Emerson will relent. I should hate to think I could never see my grandchildren. But do not write, or try to get in touch, for he will be angry for a very long time."

"You know he cannot be normal, don't you, Mama? Not and behave as he has?" Tory dared to say.

"Oh, I have always known he's never been quite sane where you were concerned. But he is my husband, and I love him regardless of that, or of anything he has done. Keep Rockford far away from him. He intends to kill him, you know."

As Tory inhaled sharply, she patted her hand and said, "Enough. Dress warmly. There is a chill breeze tonight. You can use the front door if you are quiet. Everyone is asleep."

Wordlessly, Tory stood up when her mother did and put her arms around her. She closed her eyes as they embraced, savoring the lavender scent Mary Emerson wore that would all her life bring her mother to mind. That lady put her aside then, and she did not look back before she closed the door behind her.

Tory did not waste a minute after Mary Emerson left her. She felt a great need for haste, as if even now, in spite of her mother's reassurances, her father might wake, get out of bed to check on her, and find the door unlocked. Hurriedly she emptied one of the portmanteaus and repacked it with necessities. Then she put on her bonnet and a warm dark shawl, hung her reticule over her arm, and, candle in hand, cautiously opened the door.

It was very quiet. So quiet she could hear the grandfather clock two flights down, ticking away with its distinctive wheeze. She edged towards the stairs, trying to remember any creaking boards. When she stepped on one, she froze, not even daring to breathe. But no door was thrown open, and no one called out, and quickly now, she almost ran down the stairs. She had to put down her portmanteau to undo the bolts of the front door. She wanted to hurry, but she made herself slide them back slowly, so they would make no sound. It seemed an age before she was on the front stoop, closing the door softly behind her.

Only then did she wonder how on earth she was to get to Anne's house. It was so late the street was empty, and there were no cabs abroad. She supposed she would have to walk, cringing a little at the prospect. London streets were not safe at night, not even for a man. How could she hope to travel through them without being robbed or worse? She did not know. She only knew she had to be gone from South Audley Street quickly. Hunching her shoulders as she crept down the steps and scuttled across the sidewalk, she almost felt her father at his window above her, heard it opening, and his bellow ordering her to stop, before he sent the fleetest footman flying after her. And then . . .

"Psst! miss," that high light voice she remembered whispered from somewhere nearby. Tory was so startled, she dropped her portmanteau. It hit the pavement with a terribly loud thud. Her heart pounding furiously, she turned to see in what faint starlight there was, Nicholas's tiger.

"How you frightened me!" she said, hand to her thudding heart.

"I'm sorry," he said contritely.

"What are you doing here so late at night?" she asked next.

He bent to pick up her portmanteau. "Best we be on our way, miss," he said cheerfully. "You never know who might come along, right? As for why I'm here, well, I thought I'd better keep watch over you, like. I saw an older gent across the street from Lady Garen's today, watching the house and looking cross as a boiled owl, too. But I couldn't get my guv to do anything about him."

"I am so glad to see you, Toby!" Tory exclaimed as they set out. "I had no idea how I was to get to my cousin's alone. I'm not even sure the two of us can do it.

"Hark! Do I hear voices?"

They had almost reached the corner, and the tiger stopped for a second. Then he nodded. "It's just some peep o' day boys wending their way home, miss. We'll go this way so they don't bother us."

Dutifully Tory followed the tiger through the dark streets, never questioning the direction he took, or the times he made her hide, once behind a tree, in a dark doorway another time. A few men passed them, some quiet and furtive, others drunken and boisterous, but no one saw them. It was as if they were invisible. Tory was tired when they finally reached Arlington Street, for she had never come here on foot before, and certainly never by such a circuitous route.

"Here we are, then," Toby said with his wide grin as he set down her portmanteau and gave the knocker a mighty crash. He had to sound it many more times before Lady Garen's butler's querulous voice wafted down from an attic window, demanding to know who was there.

Toby nodded in satisfaction when the butler said he would be down directly. "That's all right and tight, then," he said. "I'll be off to fetch my master, miss. Best you leave London as soon as ever may be. The carriage can come after. We'll take the phaeton and the roans. There's not a team in England can catch us, not behind them. And by tomorrow night, you'll be safe; just see if you aren't."

The door opened then, and Tory said, "Thank you, Toby. You are an angel."

"Aww," the boy said, ducking his head in embarrassment.

But when she turned again after greeting the bemused butler, Toby had already disappeared.

Sixteen

LADY GAREN ROUSED her household before she took Tory away to the privacy of her own room.

The story her cousin had to tell took some time, and Tory was in tears before it was over.

"I tell you, Anne, I had no idea my mother felt that way about me," she concluded, wiping her eyes on the handkerchief Anne gave her. "All those years, resenting me, and I never knew."

"I imagine she loved you as well," Anne pointed out. "And I don't think it was a matter of 'all those years.' Her bitterness probably only started when you grew into such a beautiful young lady, and your father's obsession worsened. Of course it must have been galling for her to have to take second place to a child, but I don't believe Aunt Mary is like some older women who can't abide having any fresh, young thing around them. No, indeed."

"I hope things will go well for her now," Tory said, mopping her eyes again. "I am so grateful to her for arranging my escape, I cannot tell you. And to think Nicholas's tiger was waiting outside the house to guide me here. It is almost like a miracle, don't you think?"

She yawned then, and Anne Garen rose. "I must have a few words with my servants, Tory," she said.

"Why don't you stretch out on my bed and try to sleep a little? You have a long day ahead of you."

Tory protested she was sure she would not even be able to close her eyes, but when Anne returned from the dressing room minutes later, she was fast asleep. She went up to the bed to stare down at her. What a beautiful girl Victoria Emerson was, she thought, without a bit of envy. And so young, too, to be able to sleep like a baby when she was still in such danger. Anne realized Tory felt safe now she had reached her cousin's house, but she knew better. Reminded of this, she hurried downstairs to the basement kitchen where she knew her servants had assembled.

There were not many of them, for she kept only a small household. The butler, a cook, two maids, and a young boy who served in a number of capacities—carrying coal, running errands, polishing boots.

They were all seated around the kitchen table, but they rose when she entered. She smiled at them.

"I know you are aware something very unusual is afoot," she began. "I would explain it to you so you will see how serious it is. As Mr. Hawes has surely told you, my cousin has just arrived. She is in flight from her parents. Yes, I know that is unfortunate, but believe me, there is an excellent reason. She has sought sanctuary here, and I intend to give it to her until her fiancé can take her away from town. But I do expect my uncle to come here looking for her, and he will be very, very angry."

The old butler looked a little apprehensive, and knowing he would bear the brunt of Gerald Emerson's blustering, Anne said, "No, do not be concerned, Hawes. There is nothing he can do. And even if he insists on searching the house, I expect Miss Emerson will be gone from it by that time. But for my safety, you must all pretend she never came here at all. Can you do that? I doubt he will question you separately, but there is always the possibility. And aiding a girl to run away from her home is a serious charge. One I do not want laid to my door."

"I never even saw a young lady," Cook volunteered. "Doris and Mae didn't, either; why, not even Bert there, so we couldn't say a word about it, m'lady."

All eyes turned to the old butler, and he stiffened. "I do assure you, ma'am, my lips are sealed. *What* young lady? *Here?*"

This stalwart declaration was ruined somewhat by the way he started and paled as the knocker began an impatient tattoo above them.

Anne Garen looked out the areaway window. There was no trace of dawn yet.

"Go and answer the door, Hawes," she said. "That cannot be my uncle, not yet. No, it will be the Marquess of Rockford, come for his bride."

The maids sighed in unison. Coo, it was just like a story out of a book, Doris thought.

"Her pa could boil me in oil, and I'd not tell," she declared, looking militant.

"I rather doubt he will be bringing any of that with him," Anne Garen said dryly. Eyeing Doris's ample frame, she added, "And if he should ask Cook to boil some up, she must simply tell him we don't have enough on hand or a big enough pot."

As she left the kitchen, she heard the servants begin to laugh, and she felt a little better. They were loyal. They would stand by her.

She found an impatient Marquess of Rockford

pacing up and down the drawing room, his top hat in his hand. He made no comment about the state of her undress, although he himself was complete to a shade. She wondered how he had accomplished that so early in the morning.

"She is here? She is all right?" he demanded.

"Do sit down, m'lord. Yes, she is here, and she has taken no harm from her adventure." Quickly she gave him the details of Tory's imprisonment and release. She did not, however, mention that Gerald Emerson had struck her. Rockford might insist on calling the man out, if you could do such a thing to your future father-in-law, and she wanted him gone. But men were so impossible with their codes of honor, their strict adherence to the rules of chivalry, which she herself thought not only antiquated but misplaced.

"You are driving your fastest team, sir?" she asked next. "I expect my uncle on my doorstep not long after dawn."

"They are harnessed to my racing curricle. Toby has them in charge."

"I suggest you do something special for that young man," Anne told him. "He was Tory's savior, you know. Without him, I doubt she could have reached me safely."

"I know. I intend to," he said, sounding impatient.

Anne smiled to herself. "I'll go and fetch Tory now. She fell asleep, worn-out with all this drama, but it is time you were both on your way. I do not even suggest you stay long enough to break your fast."

"You're right," he agreed. "Hurry, m'lady!"

"It will be all right, you know," Anne said serenely. "I realize you're concerned for her, but somehow I am sure it will all work out just fine."

When Anne shook her gently, Tory woke feeling confused. But reminded of the danger she was in, and informed Nicholas Sinclair was waiting for her below, she was quick to leave the bed.

"How wrinkled I am!" she exclaimed, looking down at her crushed, limp skirts. She was still wearing the muslin gown she had worn the previous afternoon, and now it was much the worse for the hours she had spent in it.

"There is no time to fuss over your appearance, Tory," Anne told her, holding the door to the hall open. "Hurry now, go to your Nicholas, and God speed you both!"

Tory kissed her quickly, then the two went down the stairs to where the marquess waited. He did not seem to notice his bride's less than immaculate appearance as he took her hand in his and smiled down at her, Anne thought.

"There is one thing, m'lady," Sinclair said to her, frowning now. "The license I arranged for has not come. I expect it by special messenger either today or early tomorrow. I've left a note for Bart Whitaker concerning it. Perhaps you would be so kind as to remind him we will need it at Tye for our wedding? Without it, we'll be forced to resort to the reading of the banns, and I would not have Victoria subjected to living with me unwed for three long weeks."

"I shall take care of it," Anne Garen assured him. After another hug from her cousin, and Rockford's fervent thanks for all her assistance, the two were gone. Anne lingered on the doorstep to see the curricle set off down the street, that peculiar looking but excellent tiger clinging to the back. As she turned to reenter the house, she saw there was just the faintest lightening of the sky to the east.

Closing the door, she smiled. To think that Rockford, who had had heaven knows how many mistresses in his keeping should show such concern for his bride's reputation, augured well for the future. Well, she told herself as she went upstairs again, they always say there's no one so strict as a reformed rake. For Tory's sake, I hope that is so.

Gerald Emerson arrived a bare half hour later. Anne let him cool his heels in her drawing room a good ten minutes before she came down, clutching her dressing gown and looking confused.

"Why, Uncle, what can it be that brings you here at dawn?" she asked as she entered. "Pray do not tell me my aunt has taken ill."

"Stop that," he roared. She looked him up and down coldly. He, at least, didn't look at all well. It was obvious he had dressed any which way in his haste to get here, for his jacket sat oddly on his shoulders, his cravat was a mere travesty of a gentleman's neckwear, and his heavy, florid face was unshaven.

"Where is she?" he demanded. "I'll have the answer now, and no trying to bamboozle me!"

Anne went to take a seat near the empty fireplace. "I assume you mean my cousin Tory, Uncle?" she asked. "I cannot imagine Aunt Mary coming here at this hour."

"Aye, I mean my daughter! She ran away from the house last night, and I well know this is where she would run to. But I'm her father and have full authority over her, and I tell you I'll not have this—this defiance! I see how it is now. I've been too lenient with the girl over the years, but she's

191

about to discover how harsh a disciplinarian I can be. Now, go and fetch her without further ado."

"But she is not here," his niece said evenly. "If you do not believe me, you are welcome to search the house."

Emerson's suspicious face settled into disappointment, for he knew if Anne Garen offered such a thing, there was no chance his daughter was still here.

But he was sure she *had* been, and as he smote his forehead with his fist, he exclaimed, "She's been spirited away by that rakish knave! But I'll find her, and when I do, I'll have her back where she belongs. With me.

"No doubt you think you've been very clever, don't you, my fine lady? Outsmarting me and all? But I expected something like this, and I've already sent men running to all the post roads leading out of London. At this hour of the morning, it shouldn't be at all difficult to discover the direction they took. I don't imagine many men in sporting carriages leave town at dawn with beautiful girls beside them, do you? And I'll be after them in a flash, for I must catch them up before nightfall—I must! He's not going to be allowed to ruin my precious, precious girl! No, indeed! And after I have him thrashed to within an inch of his life, I'm going to take great pleasure in killing him."

Anne Garen made herself yawn as she rose. "Are you?" she asked. "But I find I am not a bit interested in your bloodthirsty plans, Uncle. And it really is much too early for melodrama.

"Ah, Hawes. Show my uncle out. Give you good day, sir."

Anne Garen had another gentleman caller that

morning, but this one was welcomed much more warmly than her last had been.

Bart Whitaker joined her in her morning room at her invitation. She was still at breakfast, and she ordered more coffee, muffins, and shirred eggs for him as he took his seat.

"I cannot tell you how delighted I am you have come to me," she said, smiling warmly. "We have a great many plans to make."

He chuckled. "I have been inundated with things I must do today. Imagine my surprise when I woke to find I had received the most frantic, disjointed note from Rockford. Is it true, then? Did Tory run away from home? And are they gone?"

"Three hours ago," she told him.

He looked at her seriously. "Your uncle has been here?" he asked, his voice colder.

"Indeed, but there is no need to look so bleak, sir. I could hardly ask him to delay until you were here to defend me, you know. Besides, outside of a great deal of loud posturing there was nothing he could do, for Tory had left before he arrived. It does worry me a bit that he is determined to go after them, however. Pray Rockford has no trouble with his rig."

"Is he apt to dog their heels for long? I believe it takes at least two days to reach Tye."

"From something he said, I suspect if he fails to reach Tory by nightfall, he may well give up the chase." Bart looked a question, and she added, "You see, she will be ruined indeed if she is not restored to his tender care by then."

He snorted, and carefully not looking at her, he said, "I have often wondered why darkness has such a lot to do with a girl's downfall. The deed is as easily accomplished in broad daylight, after all."

"Stop trying to shock me, my old friend," she said, although her voice quivered a little as she did so. "I cut my eyeteeth years ago, and I have been married as you know."

"Yes, you have, and to my sorrow, not to me."

There was a little pause before she spoke again. "Bart? Please say no more on that head. I am sure you understand why."

He sighed. "Yes, I do, but I can wish you were not so adamant against marriage, Anne, can't I? It was my dream when we were younger, but you would have nothing to do with me."

"I was always glad you were my friend," she told him. "But it was not merely you. I didn't want to marry my husband, either, but my father insisted. But come, let's not discuss this further. What's done is done, and there is nothing you can do to change me, you know.

"Now, tell me what else the marquess asked you to do, besides deliver that all-important special license to him."

Bart took a moment to collect himself, but then to her relief he said easily, "I am to get myself to Rundle and Bridges to select the most beautiful wedding ring I can find. One that not only has diamonds, but emeralds to match Tory's eyes. I don't think there are any stones that shade, but I'll do my best. I was also ordered to procure a wardrobe for the lady, which is one of the reasons I called on you, to beg your assistance. Rockford must have been distracted indeed, to trust me to pick out shifts and gowns and nightrobes! To say nothing of something suitable for the bride to wear at her wedding."

Anne chuckled as she poured them both another

cup of coffee. "Never fear. I shall visit the shops shortly."

He had been lounging back in his chair, but now he leaned forward and said, "Anne, what is there to stop us from going to Tye ourselves? We could take the clothes, the ring, even the license with us, and then we'd be there for the wedding. Surely Tory deserves to have one member of her family with her on that important day. And as much as she loves Rockford, she is sure to be more at ease if you are there."

Anne Garen stared at him as a smile began deep in her eyes before it spread to her mouth. "But what a splendid idea," she said. "Yes, we must do that, as soon as we have finished the chores we have been set.

"Have you your carriage waiting, Bart? I'm for Bond Street!"

Miles away, Tory Emerson clung to the seat of Nick Sinclair's racing curricle as they tore through the golden morning. London had been left far behind, and the air here was fresher, cleaner. She took deep breaths of it, admiring the scenery as it flashed by.

"Have to rest the team soon, guv," Toby's high voice pronounced from behind her.

"I know. I've a mind to stop in the next village that has an inn. We've made good time, and Miss Emerson needs some food and a rest."

He looked at her where she sat so close beside him, and she smiled at him.

"Might be better if we left the post road for that, guv," Toby persisted, interrupting the fond glances his master and Miss Emerson were exchanging. "Don't forget her pa is apt to come after her, if he can discover which way we went. And since Tye is your nearest estate, I don't imagine he'll have much trouble figuring out where we're off to."

Tory paled. "Oh, let us keep going!" she exclaimed. "I do not need any food, truly, I don't."

"Well, I do, and so does Toby, to say nothing of the condition of the team. Don't worry, my dear. Your father'll not take you from me now."

"There's a crossroad up ahead, guv," Toby interrupted again. Nick Sinclair told himself he must remember how grateful he was to the tiger for his part in saving Victoria, but he really wished him at Jericho now. It was hardly a romantic elopement, with him clinging to the perch behind, listening to every word, and interpreting every glance.

They stopped at a small village a few miles farther on. Tory was glad to get down and stretch her tired muscles, as well as have the privacy of a bedchamber to freshen up in. But she was anxious until the marquess said they could be on their way again, and she often glanced over her shoulder as if she expected to see her father's carriage lumbering after them, with him seated up beside the coachman, brandishing a whip and yelling threats.

Sometime later that afternoon, she looked behind her for perhaps the hundredth time and saw how dramatically the sky had darkened to the north. It looked almost like night there, and as she watched, jagged bolts of lightning rent the sky, followed by distant rumbles of thunder, long and ominous. What was incongruous about the storm was that the weather they were enjoying was so perfect, with clear blue skies that hadn't a cloud in them.

Tory was very glad they were not caught in a thunderstorm of such massive proportions, as she pointed out the phenomena to her traveling companions.

"I've never seen anything quite like that before," Rockford said. "I hope it's not moving south. I don't want you to suffer a drenching."

"Not to worry, guv," Toby piped up. "I think that there storm is just local-like. It won't bother us none. In fact, I don't think anything more will bother us, not now."

"We must hope your optimism is not misplaced," Rockford said shortly before he turned to Tory to ask her if she were growing weary.

Behind them, Toby smirked to himself. It certainly was amusing to see how carefully his master took care of the girl, how concerned he was for her comfort. Whoever would have thought it?

They stopped for the night in a village near Faversham. The inn there was small, but it was clean, and Tory had a room to herself. She had thought she might feel awkward, alone with the marquess after dark, but he did nothing to cause her any embarrassment. Still, perverse as she was, she missed his fervent kisses and longed for him to take her in his arms.

Seated together over the remains of their dinner, to which they had done full justice, she watched him as he poured himself another glass of port. Looking up, he caught her at it, and he smiled.

"Are you content, Victoria?" he asked softly. "I am more sorry than I can say that you must go to your wedding like this."

She reached out to take his hand. "Don't be sorry; I'm not," she told him. "I think it's a wonderful adventure, and just think what an exciting tale we'll have to tell our grandchildren someday."

He raised a brow then, and she blushed, adorably

to his besotted eyes. "Time you were in bed, love. We've another long day ahead of us tomorrow," he said, rising to draw out her chair.

Standing close beside him, Tory looked up at him, her lips parting slightly. "Yes, I know," he said in a suddenly husky voice. "I want you so. It is very hard for me, harder than you know, not to love you tonight. But I am determined to wait till we are wed. You deserve such honor, and you shall have it."

Tory wished she had the courage to tell him she didn't care for that particular honor, she wanted him, too, but a huge yawn overcame her then, and when he laughed at her, the tempting moment passed.

Seventeen

THEY REACHED TYE late the following afternoon. True to Toby's prediction, no storms marred the way, nor did an irate Gerald Emerson disturb their peace. Even Tory began to feel more at ease.

She fell in love with Tye at first sight, exclaiming over the view to the sea, the fields and fruit trees, the welcoming old house sitting among its old-fashioned walled gardens like some comfortable grandmother, secure and well-loved. And she was taken with the wide center hall that stretched the depth of the house to the terrace, the shining, well-cared-for furnishings, the family portraits.

Nick introduced her to his butler as the future Lady Rockford, and instructed the man to see the best bedroom was made ready for his bride at once. Leaving him to see to that and to a tea tray, he took Tory on a tour of the ground floor.

"Of course you will want to make changes," he told her, his arm tight around her once they were alone. "I am not a great hand at decor."

"But it is perfect just as it is, Nicholas," she protested. "Well, I did notice the hangings in your library have faded somewhat, and perhaps the dining room chairs should have new coverings, but really . . ."

He laughed. "I knew your use of the word 'perfect' was only a sham, love! What woman does not want to set her own seal on her home? And then there are two others for you to change, including a very impressive main seat in Wiltshire. But come, I'm sure tea has been brought to the drawing room by now. I'm thirsty, aren't you? Afterward, you will want to change before dinner. Perhaps you'd enjoy a bath to get rid of the dust of the road? I'll introduce you to my housekeeper shortly. She's a nice woman. I'm sure you'll like her."

Tory was happy to discover she did like the motherly soul who took her to her room later, and begged her to ask for anything she needed. And after that wonderful hot bath and a short nap, she felt a new woman. Going to the window that overlooked the gardens and the channel beyond, Tory stared out to sea. There were a few sails on the horizon, and she closed her eyes, savoring the mingled aromas of flowers and salt air and damp, rich earth. She was more than content, she was happy, although she felt more than a pang whenever she thought of her mother, and she still regretted the man her father had revealed himself to be. And she missed Anne a little, too, she realized as she dressed for dinner with the help of one of the upstairs maids, hoping the clothes Nicholas had said were coming from London would not be long delayed. She had been able to bring so few of her own.

Of course she loved Nicholas to distraction, and could hardly wait to wed him, but somehow in the interim, she was alone. By herself for the first time in her life. Certainly not a wife, but somehow not a maid, either. She was not sure she liked it.

Much later that evening, after Tory had gone reluctantly to bed alone, Nicholas Sinclair sat by himself in the library, a snifter of brandy set on the small table by the side of his chair. He was not working on estate matters, or reading. Rather he was staring into the small fire that had been lit to take the damp chill from the night air, and thinking of his Victoria. It had been agony to kiss her good night and watch her go up the stairs alone, when he longed so to be with her. He wondered exactly when the special license would arrive. He intended to speak to his vicar tomorrow, of course, to alert him to the ceremony he would be required to conduct.

He was just wondering if there was any chance the license might arrive by late tomorrow when he heard Toby's voice behind him and he turned. The boy stood just inside the door of the library, and when he saw he had his master's attention, he came forward.

"What are you doing here, Toby?" Nick asked. "I didn't hear you knock."

"Because I didn't," the lad said without his usual cheeky smile. "I have come to say good-bye to you."

"Good-bye?" Nicholas echoed, frowning now and not looking a bit pleased even as he wondered why Toby seemed different to him somehow. Older, more assured, if that were possible. Even his voice was deeper, his choice of words more adult.

"Yes, it's time I went back," Toby explained. "I'm not needed here anymore, now you've found Miss Emerson and everything has worked out."

"You're going back? Where? To the country where I found you, you mean? But you said you had no ties there. Besides, I do so need you. You're the best tiger I've ever had, why, you've a way with horses that I've never seen before. And if it's a matter of money, I'm sure we can work something out."

Toby chuckled, sounding thoroughly amused. "No, it's nothing to do with money. What use is money to me? And I'm not going back to where you found me. I'm going back where I came from."

"And where is that?" Nick demanded. "You must be more plain with me."

"I'm going to heaven," Toby told him. "You see, I'm an angel."

There was complete silence in the library. Even the crackling sound of the flames as they licked at the apple logs had ceased.

Nick Sinclair stared at the redheaded lad. His round face, covered with freckles, wore an open, honest expression. But could he really believe what he was saying, or had he suddenly lost his wits? Nick decided to humor him.

"You are, are you?" he said mildly. "Well, that is certainly a surprise to me. But perhaps I should tell you, Toby, I don't believe in angels."

Toby nodded. "I know you don't. Nor in heaven or in hell, either. You don't even believe in God the Almighty. It's a pity, when you are such a sensible, knowledgeable man otherwise. But it's been my experience that sometimes human beings have little faith, the poor misguided things. But maybe from now on you'll believe."

"*Your* experience, eh? You don't look old enough to have had much of that," Nick scoffed.

Toby smiled at him. "You'd be absolutely astounded if you knew how old I really am. In fact, I don't remember myself. Aeons and aeons is the closest I can come to it."

Rockford stared at his brandy. Perhaps he was imagining all this? Perhaps Toby wasn't here at all?

"No, you're not in your cups," the boy told him. "And I am most certainly here."

"Well, let us assume you are speaking the truth," Nick went on, conversationally. "You don't look like an angel, though. In fact, you're the sorriest specimen of angelhood I can imagine."

"Not like the ones you've seen in paintings and sculpture? The ones with halos of light and big white feather wings and long white nightgowns? No, I guess I don't. But an angel can assume any shape or form, you know. Male, female—it doesn't matter. Last time I came to earth as a Chinese empress."

"Really? How interesting. I suppose you're going to claim to be my guardian angel?"

"No, not yours. I'm on loan, as it were, from someone else. Someone who loves you very much. Someone who worried about you and prayed for you so hard, there wasn't anything to do but come down here and straighten you out. Prayers can summon angels, you know. Call us down. And that's exactly what your great-aunt, Martha Lincoln, did. You should be grateful to the dear lady."

"Why did you have to come? Why didn't my own guardian angel take care of it?" Nick asked, wondering if he were going as mad as his tiger appeared to be, to be asking such insane questions.

"Well, to tell you the truth, your angel was busy with something else. Even a guardian angel has quite a lot to do. You're not his only concern. But, of course, being human and as selfish and conceited as humans almost always are, naturally you'd think you must be. I understand.

"And we often help each other out when we get pressed, even though there are such legions of us, to say nothing of archangels, principalities, powers, dominions, thrones, cherubim, and seraphim. Er, I'm afraid angels are at the bottom of the heavenly host. But it's all right. I was glad to be of assistance."

"I see. You know I don't believe a word of your story, Toby. I think you've been into the brandy somehow, and I can't say I care for it."

"I could do something that would make you believe in me, but I rather scorn parlor tricks. No angel likes them. They are a bit beneath us, don't you see? But if you'll just think back, you'll stop doubting. Remember the night we met? When you had that accident with the team and your tiger Henry was injured? How do you suppose that happened? And why?"

"You'd have me believe *you* frightened the horses? Well, I can see how that might be. But if you're an angel, how could you let that poor boy get hurt so badly? No, it doesn't make sense."

Toby threw out his hands. "Yes, that was unfortunate," he said. "But it had to be done if I was ever going to be able to get close to you. And I knew Henry never really liked being a tiger. And he hated London. He's a farmer at heart, is Henry, and he's as happy as he can be in the country. Got taken in by one of the locals who doesn't have a son. Believe me, he's not a bit sorry there was an accident."

Nick told himself there was no proof there. It could very well have happened without heavenly intervention, and he was sure it must have.

"Then, there was your sudden streak of good luck, gambling," Toby went on. "I can't tell you how amused I was when that was attributed to Iblis. Er, you know him as Satan, Prince of Darkness, and believe me, *he* didn't have a thing to do with it."

"You are saying *you* brought me good luck? *You* were the reason I could not lose?"

"Of course. I had to see to that before you found yourself ruined. It was one of the main reasons dear Martha wanted help, and prayed so hard for it."

"If I were to play again, would my luck continue?"

Toby smiled at him pityingly. "Well, you can put it to the test if you want to. But I can't imagine why you would. Now."

Changing the subject, he continued, "Then, there was the time we were coming here to Tye, and you were challenged to a curricle race. I knew the bridge railings would go, so I made you pull over. Angels can see the future, you know. There were a lot of other incidents, which you did not even notice. Lucy's convenient new protector, my knowing about your mare, Lia. Even my being able to see a packet on the horizon that day at the beach here. And how do you think it came about that I just happened to be outside Miss Emerson's house two nights ago when she ran away from her father? A coincidence? Too many of those, if you think about it.

"But let it go. You weren't there. However, you did see that black thunderstorm yesterday, the one that didn't come anywhere near us, didn't you? I arranged it to keep Miss Emerson's father from coming here and making trouble. She wouldn't have liked it if you'd shot her father. Of course, she'd be miserable if he shot you. Er, I'm afraid it was necessary to arrange for Mr. Emerson to have an accident, too. He'll be laid up for quite a while, so you don't have to worry about him anymore."

"I think you have gone mad," Nick said, looking stunned. "Either that or I have."

Toby chuckled. "No, you're not mad. And I'm certainly not."

"If you are an angel, why didn't you assume some handsomer form?" Nick asked, looking the tiger up and down.

"I could have, but I didn't. I thought it would be easier to gain your trust as a brash, freckle-faced boy. Originally I did consider becoming your valet, but I didn't because I didn't want to displace your Mr. Danby. He has a sick mother to care for, and your dismissal of him would have been hard on her. Besides, as a valet I wouldn't be able to be with you, or out of the house as often as a tiger would. And that was important."

He moved forward and reached in his pocket for a handful of coins that he put on the table beside the brandy. "Here's the money you've given me. I don't need it where I'm going. Silly thing, money, yet you humans set so much store by it. And then you give no thanks for the things that are most important—your lives, love, friendship, compassion. No, not even for the air you breathe, the food you eat, your shelter and drink, to say nothing of our heavenly Father's tender mercies toward you. If I weren't an angel and incapable of it, I'd be disheartened by the human race. They are all of them such ingrates! Well, maybe my unforgiving nature tells you why I'm still only an angel."

He shook his head and stepped back. Nick looked down at the small pile of coins beside him. Could it be that Toby was telling the truth? Could he *really* be an angel?

"Yes, I really could. I am," the boy said, reading his mind. Nick Sinclair started, then picked up his snifter and drained it.

"And I suppose you're going to tell me you made

me fall in love with Victoria?" he demanded, reminded suddenly of the girl he loved.

"Oh, no, you did that all on your own. Not that all of us weren't as pleased as could be when it happened. Because you needed someone to love, someone who could help you forget your family; mourning them the way you've been doing."

"I do not care to discuss my family," Nick said stiffly.

"I know. You can't bear to have that particular wound touched. But it's time to stop mourning, and time to remember instead all the good things about them that you loved. They all wish you would— your mother, your father, and your sister. It makes them sad that you're still so bitter about what happened."

Nick started to rise, furious, until he remembered what Toby was claiming, and he sank back into his chair again.

"Just as well you thought twice about thrashing me. Remember the fight I had in the stable in London with Jemmy, who is so much bigger and stronger than I?

"Well, best I be on my way," he added. "I've been gone too long, but all this took much more time than I thought it would."

"I still don't believe in angels," Nick muttered, never taking his eyes from his tiger, or—or whatever he was.

Toby sighed. "I know. But we have great hopes for you, Nicholas Alastair John Sinclair. Good-bye. We will meet again, you know, in heaven."

As he watched, Nick saw the boy's slight figure waver for a moment before it disappeared. In its place was only a soft, glowing light that faded even as he looked at it.

Eighteen

BY MORNING, NICHOLAS Sinclair had convinced himself he had imagined the whole thing. Of course it was true Toby was nowhere to be found, either in the barns or the stables. The little pile of his livery that had been placed on the end of his bed in the cottage where the grooms slept was all that remained of him. But still, Sinclair told himself, the story he had heard had to have been just a figment of his imagination. He might even have dozed off in his chair and dreamed it. Or perhaps he had had too much of the sherry cream sauce the crayfish had been served in, and it had affected his digestion? There were any number of logical explanations for it. Because, of course, there was no such thing as angels.

He took Tory for a long drive that morning to show her the local sights in the neighborhood. She did not remark on Toby's absence, nor did he, for he had decided the best thing he could do was forget the entire, unnerving experience.

Lady Garen and Bart Whitaker arrived the following day, the carriage they came in heaped with band boxes and parcels that contained all the clothes Anne had bought for her cousin. She and Tory disappeared upstairs to try on the wedding gown, and Rockford carried Bart Whitaker away to the village to deliver the special license and make arrangements with the vicar for a ten o'clock private service the following morning.

Tye hummed with activity as preparations for the wedding were set in train. Maids ran up and down the stairs on various errands, giggling and whispering to each other, the footmen moved furniture and polished silver, and the gardeners brought in armfuls of flowers to decorate all the rooms. Wonderful aromas began to issue from the kitchen in anticipation of the wedding breakfast the marquess had invited all his neighbors to, immediately following the ceremony. And with all the activity afoot, Sinclair was able to put Toby and his ridiculous claim from his mind.

But that evening as the four of them sat at dinner, Anne Garen suddenly said, "Oh, to think it should have slipped my mind in the excitement! I must tell you, Tory, your father has met with an accident."

Nick Sinclair's fork clattered against his plate, but no one noticed as Tory cried out, "How did it happen? Do tell me he was not seriously injured!"

"Don't worry," Bart reassured her. "He has only broken his leg, and if he can be persuaded to remain quiet for the necessary weeks, he is expected to make a full recovery. As for how it happened, well, that was strange. He was hot behind you and Sinclair, intent on catching you up, when he had the bad luck to find himself in a bad thunderstorm. The coachman insisted on stopping until it was over, and Mr. Emerson impatiently got down to remonstrate with him before the groom could position the steps. It was slippery, and he must have tripped, for he fell heavily to the road. There was nothing to be done but take him back to London and a doctor.

"Well, I am sure we are all glad he did not stop you both, but I must say it was really the worst kind of luck. You see, the storm, although unbelievably severe, was limited in area. We were told that not five miles away, the sun continued to shine throughout its entire duration. Rather like being in the wrong place at the wrong time with a vengeance, eh?"

No, Nick Sinclair told himself. It was just another coincidence, nothing more. He would not believe otherwise, damn it!

That night when he said good night to Tory, he did so with a lighter heart, for this was the last night they would have to spend apart. He knew she was thinking of that as well, for when her clear green eyes met his, she flushed a little and lowered her lashes to hide them. He bent to whisper his love for her in her ear before he sent her up the stairs after one last fervent embrace.

He was disappointed the next morning to discover the lovely June weather they had been enjoying had disappeared. The skies were a leaden gray, and rain splattered continuously on the window-panes, while a brisk wind ruffled the channel. It was really too bad that his Victoria had to have such a downpour on her wedding day, Sinclair told himself as he deftly tied his cravat, but there wasn't anything he could do about it, more's the pity. What a shame Toby hadn't really been an angel! If he had, he could have produced a beautiful day.

But when his bride came down the stairs later to join him, dressed in a cream silk gown trimmed with matching lace and ribbons, and wearing a glorious bonnet to match, he forgot all about the weather. She was so beautiful she took his breath away. And he found himself hoping he would be worthy of her, this girl who thanked him for his bouquet of yellow roses, and smiled at him so radiantly, this lovely girl who was willing to take the most dangerous gamble of all, entrusting her life to him. He promised himself he would never disappoint her if he could possibly help it.

Anne Garen watched him and smiled to herself. When she saw Bart Whitaker looking at her, she nodded to him, her face serene. It was going to be all right for Tory. She could tell.

The service at the village church was brief. Only Anne Garen and Whitaker attended the couple. The elderly vicar beamed as he pronounced them man and wife. Behind him, his wife played the organ softly. But just before they left the church to sign the register, Nick Sinclair looked around, bemused. He could tell the storm continued, for the rain still beat against the small leaded panes of the few windows on the sides of the church. The sound of that rain on the slate roof overhead was a constant tattoo, and he could hear the wind setting the bell up in the belfry to a soft jangling. But why, then, he wondered, had the large round stained-glass window behind the altar begun to glow as if the sun had just come out? He looked to the others, but no one else appeared to notice, for Victoria was embracing her cousin, and Whitaker was shaking hands with the vicar. As Nick watched in some trepidation, the soft reds, blues, golds, and greens of the window brightened until they formed a kaleidoscope of brilliant, tumbling color whirling in a dizzying sequence that bathed everyone's face in warmth. He closed his eyes, for it was so strong, it hurt. Even so, he could still see it. The throbbing light pierced his eyelids, as if determined not to let him go until he acknowledged it.

It was then he knew why the weather had been so miserable today, where that light was coming from, and the reason he was the only one who could see it.

"All right, Toby," he whispered, humbled and in awe. "Maybe it did take a parlor trick, but you finally convinced me. And I'll never doubt again, for I find I do indeed believe in angels. Er, that is, one particular angel anyway."